A NOTE ON THE AUTHOR

Born in Glasgow in 1936, Norman Maclean was educated at school and university there before abandoning his childhood ambition of becoming a helicopter pilot – or was it a cowboy? – and drifting into the role of educationalist and spending fourteen miserable years as a teacher of Latin and Mathematics in schools all over Scotland. He garnered much fame after winning two Gold Medals at the National Mod – for poetry and singing – in the same year, 1967; the only person ever to do so. Shortly afterwards he began a career, as he would say himself, as a clown. The twenty odd years he spent as a stand-up comedian performing in variegated venues throughout the English-speaking world has caused him to book a place on a daytime television show renowned for its shouty, self-righteous former-salesman presenter. However, that said, it is in the roles of comic and musician Maclean is still best known today. In 2009 Birlinn published his acclaimed auto-biography, *The Leper's Bell*.

Tricksters

Norman Maclean

BIRLINN

First published as *Slaightearan* in 2007 by Clàr
This edition published in 2011 by
Birlinn Limited
West Newington House
10 Newington Road
Edinburgh
EH9 1QS

www.birlinn.co.uk

ISBN 978 1 78027 007 4
eBook ISBN 978 0 85790 060 9

British Library Cataloguing-in-Publication Data
A catalogue record for this book is available from the British Library.

Designed and typeset by Iolaire Typesetting, Newtonmore
Printed and bound by Bell & Bain Ltd, Glasgow

For Alison Rae

Contents

Me, I'm from Kyles Flodda in Benbecula. Murdo, son of Boozy Ronald, they call me. Here I am, sitting on the couch in the living room of a little flat near the Shawlands district of Glasgow. It's a cold afternoon in February and I'm reading a book on Economics and making occasional notes in a folder. We have exams in six weeks' time at Strathclyde University where I'm studying Statistics, Sociology, Psychology and Industrial Law. I want to gain a Postgraduate Diploma in Personnel Management. I can hardly believe that I, an overweight slob, fast approaching forty, who smokes and drinks too much, am a full-time student once more. And I'm simply loving it! To tell the truth, I'm not as keen on the bevvy as I used to be. I still have a heavy tobacco habit but I've severely cut down on the alcohol.

The sound of the outside door being opened interrupts my reverie. Two minutes later, a beautiful young woman enters the room carrying two tiny glasses of Disaronno, an Italian liqueur we've come to enjoy very much. She sits next to me on the couch and kisses me lightly on the cheek. We both take a modest sip and politely place the glasses on a rectangular table in front of us.

This is Rachel, the Doctor's daughter, from North Uist. She's twenty years younger than me and, if we're talking about PR, there's no woman between the Butt of Lewis and

1

Barra Head who can hold a candle to Rachel MacKinnon. No matter how hard you stretch it, there is nothing within eyeshot that is better to look at. Six feet tall, long, straight hair that falls to the small of her back, the face of an angel and a well put-together body that has caused many a traffic accident – Rachel is a danger to any man with a weak heart. In addition, she's very smart. She's reading Law at Glasgow University and there's no doubt that she'll graduate with Honours in her final year.

So, here's the pair of us relaxing, taking little sips of Disaronno and chatting about how our respective days have gone at uni. Am I a lucky guy or what?

Around eight months ago things were completely different. In the summer of 2010 I would have gulped the contents of the glass as quickly as I could. Then, I'd immediately want more. For years I had been filling glasses with strong drink – whisky, Eldorado rum, brandy, wine, beer – any kind of rubbish I could get my hands on. Talk about a changed man!

But I'd better start at the beginning . . .

'We'll go on a tour of the Highlands and Islands with your sketches, Murdo, and it'll be simply marvellous.' That's what Rachel proposed at the start of last summer. Mickey the Dunce here agreed and I had no recollection of my grandfather's words: 'You want to get into trouble, son, you should get into trouble for profit, not just for self-expression.' 'Salt and Pepper' – that's what we called ourselves – went on the road and, at first, we did quite well . . . we did very well indeed . . . but . . . well . . . I kind of ran out of steam . . . I don't know . . . I . . . sort of . . . lost the plot.

On the last night of the tour, a Monday night, the night before we'd go back to Uist, we should have been playing in Broadford but . . . well, we lost the hall . . . Well, we didn't

2

lose *the hall – we know where it is, it's still in the same place – what it was, the committee wouldn't give it to us. We pressed on to Uig and landed in a hotel there called the Tartan Pagoda, and if relations between me and Rachel were fraught before this, they got really bad after I got embroiled with this guy and his television crew. There's a motto in our family and it certainly applies to me: 'If a thing is worth doing, it's worth doing wrong.'.*

There was this guy, Sam was his name, and he was in television . . . and I was in my shell-suit. I consulted my watch with all the intensity of a professor of history scrutinising a script in Sanskrit as Sam's monologue went over the fifty-minute mark. He had bought me a nip in the bar at quarter past ten, and now at a quarter to midnight, or possibly a week later, we were making our way to the dining room for a bite to eat. My jaw was aching with the effort of suppressing yawns as he went on and on and on about film locations in Uist and about acting talent and how stupid they were, and above all about money. Drams were flying, so was I, and some of the locals were pretending not to listen, and he gave every appearance of being pleased by the attention, as though he deserved it.

'Oh, yes, Our Land *was written by me,' he roared, thrusting his face close to mine and smoothing his hair in a self-satisfied manner. 'I take all the blame, ha ha. Guilty as charged. I'm only the humble author.' He obviously thought this was funny . . . I didn't. But I didn't know what I should say. Should I have told him that I was an actor, and writer, too? Should I have mentioned that I had viewed* Our Land *and would rather smear dung on my head than watch it? Or should I just concentrate on the drink until the curtain came down? My confusion wasn't helped by Sam's artificial smile, a fixed rictus that would have scared Bronson. He*

3

seemed to be waiting for me to say something, something that I had to say because he was a famous person. But since I didn't know what it was, he was obliged to keep on talking.

'But that's enough about me,' he said, and anyone could tell he wasn't finding this easy. 'Tell me what you think about me!' I was out my skull when we finally ate — me, Sam the Etive Television guy and Yvonne, his PA — in the dining room round about midnight. I kissed Yvonne's hand. I ordered champagne. The place was full of Etive Television people. I developed a case of the hiccups, more like a series of uppercuts to the chin. One of these blows actually knocked me on my arse and I had to lie on my back beneath the table until I felt a bit better. My knee brushed against Yvonne's, once, twice, and I thought how wonderful it was when two young people started to fall in love.

The following day, the twenty-fourth of August, although things started off rather painfully, what with a toxic hangover and Rachel's nagging, they gradually got better as the day went on.

1

Uig pier

24 August 2010, 9.30 a.m.

John MacNicol stood in the centre of the parking area at Uig pier in Skye waving his arms and bellowing. It was a warm and clammy morning, and sweat showed on his face and on his black shirt bearing the logo of Caledonian-MacBrayne on the breast. He was about fifty, five six. He wore heavy black boots and he stamped his feet while he roared into the kind of metal megaphone favoured by the police and this made his voice sound distorted: 'Come out of that van immediately. Hands in the air. You are surrounded . . . by other vehicles. This is . . . the Traffic Controller. Conduct of this nature will not be tolerated . . . not in the middle of a queue . . . on Uig pier!'

Rachel walked from the nearside of the van – she had been rocking the van and beating on its side – round past the bonnet and looked down contemptuously on the middle-aged Skyeman. 'Are you going to order me to throw down my handbag as well, you half-wit? I'm trying to waken the guy who's inside.'

'Oh! I thought . . .'

'Dirty old man!' Rachel said. 'What a welcome for two hard-working actors! Can't you read the writing on our van?'

5

MacNicol closely examined the writing on the side of the van. COMEDY ON TOUR – FUN AND LAUGHTER WITH SALT AND PEPPER. 'Salt and Pepper!' he said with a sneer. 'I've heard about you. Our Mary saw you in Staffin one night and she said the pair of you were going straight to Hell . . . on wheels!' With considerable difficulty he took his eyes off Rachel and glanced at the van. 'The man who's locked himself in is Salt, right?'

No sooner had he said this than Murdo made an appearance wearing cotton checked trousers of the kind much favoured by circus clowns and a baggy top of deep purple hue. He swallowed three times in succession and looked around him as though in a daze. 'Many a perilous drunk I've been on,' he intoned faintly, 'but if they were all rolled into one, this is the mother of them all.'

'By the look of him,' the Skyeman said, 'it wasn't salt that's giving him a drouth today. I'd say he was out his box somewhere last night.'

'We were in Aultbea actually,' Rachel lied smoothly. 'Last night of the tour and all that.'

'Well, you're in Skye now,' MacNicol said, 'and the ferry's due in about an hour's time. Are you sailing on her?'

'You bet, lad,' Murdo barked roughly, 'even if I have to swim out to meet her.'

'Maybe that's what you'll have to do yet, Pop,' MacNicol said with a mocking laugh, 'if you don't have tickets. Are you booked on?'

'Ah . . . we haven't . . . I'm just going over to the office right away,' Rachel said in a quivery voice.

'Right,' the Traffic Controller said, 'drive over and join that queue across there – where it says LOCAL

TRAFFIC – and you can park this old rattletrap . . . And, lassie, if I were you, I'd leave the old boy over there as well . . . in case anybody sees him. He'll give folk the horrors.'

Rachel steered over to the area designated LOCAL TRAFFIC. Murdo's moans accompanied the straining engine. Once stopped, she turned to Murdo and spoke angrily. 'Murdo, stop your whingeing, and listen carefully. I've got bad news for you and I know it's going to be painful for you to hear it.'

'Rachel, love,' Murdo said with a heavy sigh, 'I can't possibly feel much worse than I do just now.'

' "We'll see", as the blind man said,' Rachel replied.

Me, I'm from . . . ah . . . from Back in Lewis. Well, I was born in the Poligan, the only son of Effie MacMillan, but I was brought up in Inverness, Aberdeen and Perth. Sam Kerr's my Sunday name, but I much prefer the nickname they gave me when I was still quite young. That's 'Sam the Scam'. I never knew my father – some bastard from the Lowlands who abandoned his wife shortly after I was born – and my poor mother had to work in the Northern Bank in different branches where she was bored out of her skull. When I was growing up, she always used to advise me to take a secure job in a bank. She wanted, I'm sure, to ensure that her son suffered the same agony she endured. When I entered the world of television, she was not best pleased. As it turned out, her own job wasn't as secure as mine. Much of the staff at the Northern Bank was 'slimmed down', and replaced by stacks of electronic machines and computers which made a box-up of people's savings, chewed up credit cards, and charged usurious rates of interest that would have shamed the moneylenders Jesus scourged from the Temple. These machines were free to steal without any human supervision.

Never mind, here I am lying on a blanket on the pavement of a street called the Cowgate in Edinburgh. It's a cold, wet night in February, and me and a crowd of people, mostly pale-faced males with a couple of females thrown in, are waiting for the big lorry carrying the priest and a young team of boys and girls who give out sandwiches and soup to the unfortunate souls who are homeless. I can hardly believe that I, Sam the Scam, formerly Head of Drama and Documentaries at Etive Television, am now considered a member of the underprivileged.

'Homeless?' The priest is approaching with a steaming mug and a roll.

'Not for long.' I'm hoping to get back with Dolina, though she put me out of the house as soon as she discovered I'd lost my job and the days of the megabucks were long gone.

'Because we're MWH. Sorry, Meals on Wheels for the Homeless.'

'Well, yes, I suppose I am. Temporarily homeless.'

'I understand. My name's Kenneth.' The priest hands over the food. 'What's yours?'

'Donald.' The lie issues from my mouth with practised ease. All my life I've been telling lies. In IRA, or Inverness Royal Academy, and in Dundee University, where I opted for Journalism, I didn't spend much time studying. I used to cheat on teachers and lecturers, cribbing assignments from the few pals I had. This habit of deceit was extremely useful when I finally reached the world of television. It's true, if you put down on your CV that you're a self-centred bastard, it'll do you no harm at all.

I know all about this. The first thing I did when I moved from the Perthshire Gazette, *where I was a tipster for our readership who liked to gamble on the horses, to Etive Television was to wield the axe. I got rid of every producer, presenter and director in the place and hired two or three people who would do exactly as I'd tell them. This action saved the company a great deal of money, and my standing with the Board increased dramatically.*

How things have changed! I used to cut back on staff expenses and what I skimmed went into my own pocket. I was so well off that some days I couldn't remember which of my cars I'd taken to work in the morning. I'd have to go down to the car park at lunchtime and look around. 'Ah, yes,' I'd say, 'it was raining when I left home this morning. I took the red one.'

But the wheel has turned full circle and the warmth has become bitter cold.

However, I'd better start at the beginning, the summer of last year . . .

We were on our way to the Uists – my PA, Yvonne, a cameraman, soundman, a sparky and myself, Leader of the Pack – to shoot footage for a documentary called In the Footsteps of Erskine Beveridge. *We lodged in a hotel called the Tartan Pagoda on the Monday night with the intention of catching the ferry to Lochmaddy on Tuesday, the twenty-fourth of August. Although things had started off rather promisingly, it was to become my day of disaster and shame . . .*

2

To feed the flame

24 August 2010, 9.30 a.m.

Sam Kerr lay, naked, on his back, in the middle of a bed in
Room 3 in the Tartan Pagoda. His arms and legs were
stretched out in the form of an X. His head lolled on his
shoulder as though he had been garrotted. He was a large,
well-built man, twenty-eight years of age; a descendant of
a race of seamen well accustomed to extreme cold and
spray from hostile waves. His hair was long and thick,
dyed yellow, and flowed over his ears to a loosely plaited
pigtail at the back. He sported an all-over tan, for he was
seriously addicted to sun beds. The bleep of his mobile
phone awoke him. He got up, scratched his chest, pulled
on a silk bathrobe and padded into the bathroom. After
micturating, he washed his hands and put out his tongue
at the mirror above the handbasin. This tongue re-
sembled a slice of steak that had been baking in the
sun for at least a fortnight. Too many cigarettes and
drinks last night. And every night. He had a dim memory
of standing at the bar casting pearls of wisdom to Yvonne
and a pudding of a man from Benbecula, and though he
couldn't put a face to the guy, he was pretty confident
that, with his natural way with words, he had impressed

him. The retard who had been so drunk he'd tried to chat up Yvonne – what a deluded fool! He quickly erased the memory of the previous night from his mind.

This was the worst time for somebody connected to television who was about to embark on filming a programme that would certainly gain another BAFTA award and reap fame and fortune for its creator. This was the time he had to haul himself out of sleep, all alone, examine his dried-up tongue, rub his red-rimmed eyes, and finger the stubble on his jowls. He wondered, for a moment, if the game was worth the candle. To banish these depressing thoughts he decided to take a shower. When he had finished his ablutions he felt invigorated and spoke aloud: 'Rangers 3 Celtic 1. Have we visions to mix and awards to be won? Yes, Sam, baby, you certainly have!' His electric razor started to hum, and Sam's brain started to hum too. First, he'd check every part of his room for anything that he could possibly steal, and then he'd have a quick look in the holdall that contained his treasure and his heart.

Sam returned to the bedroom and dressed in clothes he considered appropriate for a director of a television crew – chinos, Timberland brogues, a white polo shirt with the logo of Etive Television on the front, and a blue baseball cap, skip to the rear, bearing the Latin legend *Alere Flammam*. He glanced at his watch. 09.40. He picked up a red canvas bag – there were at least four of them scattered around the room – and with trembling fingers opened it. He gazed with reverence at the dozens of little packets of shortbread, coffee, sugar and miniature jars of jam – the kind of snack food that can be found next to the kettle in most hotels. He whispered excitedly, 'Wonderful!'

14

Me, I'm from North Uist. To tell you the honest truth, I don't know. I don't know if there is a shred of hope for us right now. I came to a decision that he was the man I wanted, and it may have been the wrong decision, but I made the decision anyway, and here I am right here. Honestly, I don't know what can change that. I love Murdo, and I'm trying to do the honourable thing. There's either some hope in that, or there isn't.

Well . . . uh, Murdo . . . my father and mother . . . and lack of money.

Murdo's the main problem.

He's a hollow man.

He has no trade, he's almost forty years of age, he's been on the 'Out-of-Work' since he got the elbow from the university and . . . he drinks too much. Well, not so much recently. He's really made an effort. But, despite all that, he makes me laugh sometimes. What I mean is, I'm comfortable with him. I can't imagine me making it without him being in my life in some way or other.

But I don't want to hurt my parents. God, they're always giving me static because I'm going with him. Well, my father's not as heavy as her, but I know he's hurting. He's disappointed in my behaviour . . . But it's his own fault. 'Daughter of mine,' my poor dad must have said to me at an impressionable age, 'never learn from your mistakes, never

15

*pay any heed to experience. Is that clear? Also, always be
hopeful, that if you get involved with an old drunk, everything will turn out all right, even in the teeth of outright
contradictory proof. Now, all right, let's have it, what did I
just tell you?'*

*'What did you tell me?' I must have hotly replied. 'You
told me nothing! I don't need anyone to tell me anything!
What the hell are you questioning me for? My life's going to
be like a Gaelic song.' At which my daddy presumably
chuckled and said, 'That's my girl!'*

*And then my poor old white-haired mother, her and her
old black mourning gear, comes to my room looking like
somebody that just got hit in the head. And I've got to sit
through all that Gaelic psalm wailing. You know, 'Cia
fhad' a bhitheas corruich ort, a Dhè, am bi gu bràth?' 'How
long will wroth be upon you, Lord, will it be forever?' 'I
pray for you, Rachel,' she says. 'I sent a donation to the
Resuscitation Fund on your behalf. I hope you give that man
up, Rachel. I know in my heart you're a good girl.'*

*'Rachel,' she says, 'you've got to get onto the straight and
narrow.' She writes to a religious bookshop in Partick every
week and orders cassettes of famous Free Church ministers'
sermons. She's offering to send me to Lourdes . . . and we're
not even Catholic!*

'Look, Mother, I'm not crippled,' I tell her.

'In your soul you are,' she says.

*Jesus, isn't it great to be young! They disapprove of him.
They think he's too old for me, that his family are low-rent,
that I should finish my course at uni . . . and that's what
I'm going to do.*

As the old guy from Barra said, 'I'm in a quadrangle'.

*But I'd better start at the beginning, the summer of last
year . . .*

3

I know what you did in Golspie

24 August 2010, 10.15 a.m.

'I had to sleep in the van. Well, I lay down in the van. Didn't get a wink,' Murdo said, shaking like a fishing rod.

'Your conscience killing you, was it?'

'It was the cold,' Murdo said. 'I looked round, first thing this morning, to see if old Admiral Scott or Roald Amundsen were hanging about. They'd have felt right at home in this van.'

'You didn't get a bed at the party, then?'

'It wasn't up to much.'

'You didn't pull a bird, then?'

'There weren't any women there,' Murdo said.

'The cruiserweight was there!'

'Well, there was one woman called Yvonne,' Murdo said, 'who worked for that television guy . . . the guy who was buying me all the drams last night. I thought he was going to offer me some work . . . since you and I are . . . more or less, er, finished.'

'Oh, we're not quite finished yet, Murdo.'

'Anyway,' Murdo said, 'I put up a kind of black along with Yvonne and Sam.'

'Yvonne . . . She was the one in the dungarees, wasn't she?'

'Yes.'

'Timberland boots on? Peroxide hair, cropped into her head?'

'Something like that.'

'Murdo,' Rachel said with a chuckle, 'she wouldn't go with you if you were the last man on earth. She's buckled, you half-wit!'

'If I were the last man on earth,' Murdo said defiantly, 'I'd be far too busy to bother with the likes of her!'

'What a stud you are!'

'Rachel, I just thought you'd let me . . .'

'What? Stay where you are, you gimp!'

'Will you not let me get the head down in your room?' Murdo said.

'I'm going upstairs for a shower,' Rachel said. 'I reckon you'd have . . . maybe five minutes in it.'

'That's not what I meant at all.'

'I know fine what you meant,' Rachel said.

'Shall I tell you about the black I put up?' Murdo said.

'No,' Rachel said. 'I'm sick fed up of all the blacks you've put up.' She turned to face Murdo full on. 'Murdo, we've got to talk.'

'What is it you want?' Murdo said.

'I've never asked you for anything, have I?' Rachel said.

'No, you haven't,' Murdo said, 'but if you had done, I'd have done miracles for you.'

'That's good to hear, Murdo,' Rachel said. 'And I was always straight with you, wasn't I?'

'You were,' Murdo said.

'Whatever we made at the shows we put on, didn't I give you half?'

'You did.'

'I never once opened my mouth about you drinking too much.'

'No, you never did.'

'I've been a good partner to you.'

'Yes.'

'Because I could've been pretty rotten to you if I'd wanted.'

'Aye, right, just a minute, Rae . . . let me . . .'

'I could've left you in the gutter, if I'd wanted,' Rachel said. 'I know what you did in Golspie. Do you remember that night?'

'Yes!' Murdo replied vehemently. 'I remember that night.'

'That's good,' Rachel said. 'After every gig we played, I wrote down every single penny of income we made at the door. I *knew* how much should've been there.'

'Just tell me what you want.'

'Am I keeping you back from anything, Murdo?'

'I need to see somebody in the hotel.'

'Yvonne?'

'Maybe.'

'The one with the facial hair?' Rachel said.

'Now, Rachel,' Murdo said, 'there's no need for you to be so sarcastic towards me just because I made some little mistake up in Golspie.'

'Some *little mistake*?'

'Rachel,' Murdo sighed, 'I'm out on my feet here. Okay, I had a small refreshment along with . . . uh, friends, last night. That's all. I'm feeling like a raw egg in a bowl today. I'm . . . what I need is sleep, know what I mean? But all you want to do is . . .'

'Have a word with you?' Rachel said. 'You can talk

rubbish all night with your friends, but you can't spare a minute to talk to me?'

'You know I was doing some PR last night . . . so that I could get – so that *we* could get – some work.'

'Is that what you were doing?' Rachel said. 'I thought you were polishing the backsides of Yvonne and Sam. Why wouldn't you come up the stairs with me at midnight?'

'I did come,' Murdo said. 'You'd locked the door.'

'I heard you,' Rachel said. 'At four o'clock in the morning.'

'I went back downstairs again.'

'Oh!' Rachel said. 'You went down to have some more drams with your friends?'

'No,' Murdo said. 'I went to the van here. And I wasn't a happy unit about that. I was looking forward to the last night of our tour.'

'I'm sure you were,' Rachel said. She spoke solemnly: 'The Day of Judgement has arrived, Murdo.'

'What on earth are you talking about?'

'We're in a fix,' Rachel said. 'Deep in the pit of poverty, Murdo. The bottle has been . . . uh, drained . . . the fire has been doused.'

'What've . . . how much money have we got left?'

'Forty-seven pounds and fifty-three pence,' Rachel said.

'That's not much,' Murdo said.

'No, it's not,' Rachel said, 'but it's enough to . . . well, you know yourself, don't you?'

'No, I don't know,' Murdo said. 'We've enough for what?'

'There's enough to pay for the room and be out of here by twelve noon.'

20

'I was only in the room for two minutes,' Murdo said. He thought for a second. 'That means we've got two hours . . . nearly.'

'Wouldn't your teacher be proud of you today, if only he could see how slick you are at the mental arithmetic!'

'I just thought we'd plenty of time to . . .'

'To do what?'

'To . . . you know . . .'

Rachel chuckled and said, 'I don't know.'

'Well . . . to go for a wee lie down together,' Murdo said. 'Just to heat myself up. I nearly froze to death in this van.'

'If you're cold, wear long johns,' Rachel said. 'And with regard to the other thing, forget it.'

'Okay, okay,' Murdo said. 'You pay the bill . . . before noon. What'll we have left?'

'Seventeen or eighteen quid and smash,' Rachel said.

'What'll we do with that?'

'I can buy a ticket that'll take me back to Uist,' Rachel said.

'What about me?'

'You can stay here . . . along with Yvonne,' Rachel said.

'For God's sake!'

'Wrong, Murdo,' Rachel said, 'it's for your own sake.'

'How?'

'Do you want me to show you how much money we made?' Rachel said. She made to hand over a notebook.

Murdo would not even look at it. 'That's fine, Rachel,' he said airily. 'I trust you.'

'I don't trust you, though,' Rachel said. 'Do you know this, Murdo?'

'What?'

'We could've made a fortune on this tour.'

'We could have.'

'Everything went brilliantly for us at the start.'

'It did that,' Murdo said. 'I was – we were marvellous in Harris, Uist and Barra . . . aye, in Argyll and Lochaber, too . . .'

'And then something happened in Golspie,' Rachel said.

'Yeah . . . Golspie,' Murdo said.

'You don't want me to mention Golspie, do you, Murdo?'

'No.'

'Okay,' Rachel said. 'Time's wearing on. We tried to make some money from the concerts and we failed. We'll have to go down another road now. And you'll have to get shot of those rags you're wearing.'

Murdo looked down at his clothing. 'What's wrong with this gear?' After a pause, he said, 'Oh, I get it. People'll know I'm a *media person*, isn't that it?'

Rachel gave her cheek a light slap. 'When you gaze at the stars at night, Murdo, don't you ever get homesick?'

'All right, just a minute, Rae . . . let me . . .'

4

Rachel's not finished yet

24 August 2010, 10.30 a.m.

Suddenly, Rachel jumped out the van, flung open the rear door and began to rake among the clothing strewn around the floor. She threw some bits and pieces in Murdo's direction. 'Put these bits and bobs in a plastic bag,' she said. 'This is yours . . . trews . . . Balmoral bonnet . . . this tie – I think that belonged to your old man before you. Oh! The engagement ring you bought in Woolies . . . the one you tried to give me in Inverness when you were drunk . . .' She tossed a little cardboard box towards him.

Murdo failed to catch it. He had to keep on forcing scraps of clothing down into the plastic bag until, finally, he picked up the box containing the ring and carefully placed it in his pocket.

Rachel continued her recital: 'False breasts . . . drawers . . . a wig . . . Jew's harp . . .'

'Uh . . . I forgot I had so many props,' Murdo said.

'Never mind,' Rachel said, 'I've still got a good memory.'

'What do you want me to do?' Murdo said.

'Get out!' Rachel said. 'Get out of my sight!'

'You've put me off my stroke,' Murdo said, pulling a half bottle of spirits from the inside pocket of his fleece. He cracked open the cap. 'I think,' he said, 'I'll have a mouthful of this – a drop to wet my throat, know what I mean?'

Rachel seized the bottle and took it from him. 'You've just quit, Murdo.'

'I just need a charge,' Murdo said.

'Did you need one in Golspie?'

'Oh, come on, Rae,' Murdo said. 'I just don't want to start shaking like a fishing rod.'

'The shakes never killed anybody,' Rachel said.

'In Golspie it was different,' Murdo said. 'Things were coming to an end.'

'Coming to an end?'

'Between me and you,' Murdo said.

There was a long pause before Rachel spoke again. 'Murdo?'

'What?'

'Do you like me?'

Hurriedly Murdo pulled her by the shoulders to his chest. He tried to kiss her, but she pushed him away. She laughed and handed him the bottle.

'Take a sip, Murdo,' she said. 'It'll calm you down.'

Murdo refused to accept the drink.

'That's good, Murdo,' Rachel said.

Murdo sank to his knees and seemed to be on the verge of tears. 'Listen, Rae,' he said, 'I always tried to do my best for you.'

'Your best?'

'Didn't I write the comedy sketches when you wanted to go on the road?' Murdo said.

24

'But you weren't terribly good at bringing them alive onstage at the latter end.'

'I wasn't always drunk,' Murdo said. 'I did well in Tarbert, Harris, Sgoil Lianacleit in Benbecula and in Castlebay . . .'

'Golspie,' Rachel said.

'But we made it anyway,' Murdo said. 'We're still together.'

Rachel glanced at her wristwatch. 'Until two o'clock,' she said, 'at the very latest.'

'Maybe we could put on a show here,' Murdo said.

'I'm going back to Uist,' Rachel said. 'You put on a show here.'

'I don't know,' Murdo said.

'I'll tell you what your only option is,' Rachel said. 'You'll have to get hold of some money.'

'What good's that going to do?'

'Well, first of all,' Rachel said, 'I'll get my money back. Who knows? Maybe we'll make a fresh start. I just don't know.'

'I'd be – er, I *am* willing to help you, Rae, any way I can,' Murdo said. 'You must know that. I've always been fond of you. But . . .'

'*Fond?*' Rachel said. 'You're only willing because you're fucking *crazy* about me.'

'*Crazy?*'

'I know what your heart's desire is, Murdo,' Rachel said.

'What?'

'Me,' Rachel said. 'Me, Rachel. The Doctor's daughter from North Uist.'

'What do you want me to do, Rachel?' Murdo said. 'Do you want me to sell the van?' He placed a finger on his ear lobe. 'You wouldn't want me to sell my earring, would you?'

'It's just a wee notion that's come to me . . . uh, gradually, like.'

'What kind of notion?'

'Subjects like guilt and redemption,' Rachel said.

'Oh, I know nothing about those subjects, Rachel,' Murdo said. 'I only went to Torlum School. In Donald Macleod's wee blue bus.'

'Oh, you know about them all right, Murdo,' Rachel said.

'Wait a minute . . .'

'I'll wait until the ferry sails at two o'clock, if you want,' Rachel said. There was a moment of silence. Then her voice became decidedly harder. 'Why did you take the money, Murdo?'

'I hate talking about money,' Murdo said.

'Did you buy yourself new clothes – something you really needed?' Rachel said. 'No! You did what you always do. You drank it!' She stopped talking for a short while. 'And what's the particular attraction this Yvonne has for you, anyway? Do you think a big, strapping lassie like her can do some trick that no other woman can do? Do you fancy her putting a leash round your neck before you go to bed?'

'No.'

'No,' Rachel said. 'Rough handling like that wouldn't be to your taste at all. You'd rather be petted by some girl . . . you know, "drowning in the ocean of a thousand kisses".'

'Hey, that's right,' Murdo said.

'But you were never treated like that, were you?' Rachel said.

'No,' Murdo said. 'No, I wasn't.'

'Would you enjoy it,' Rachel said, 'if you and a young girl were to be kissing and fondling one another constantly? To be squeezing and stroking and tickling and sucking? Murdo, son of Winey Ronald, being along with a comely maiden with soft lips and white teeth, eh? You and . . . me, for example?'

'I think I'll have that drink now,' Murdo said.

'You'll not!' Rachel said. 'Do you know how much you owe me? You've really got to repay me, Murdo.'

'I'm off, Rae,' Murdo said.

'It's a free country,' Rachel said. 'Remember, though, unless you come back here before two with some money, you'll be left behind here on your own.' She smiled. 'And you certainly won't be "drowning in the ocean of a thousand kisses".'

'You'd leave me here without a coin in my pocket?'

'Don't you have any money?' Rachel said.

'Ten pence.'

'Do you want to stick that in with the takings?'

'No.'

'Didn't think so,' Rachel said.

'Rachel,' Murdo said, 'there's profit and loss in every business.'

'Newsflash, Murdo,' Rachel said, '*we* had a profit. *I* had an enormous loss!'

'What's all this talk about?' Murdo said. 'Is it about the cash I . . . umh, borrowed?' He remained silent for a couple of beats. 'I can't carry on like this. What'll I do for you?'

'Put the money back, Murdo!' Rachel said.

'I'm getting bored with this conversation,' Murdo said. 'This isn't about money, is it?'

'No.'

'But you're pretending it is,' Murdo said. 'That's your privilege. I'll tell you what I'm going to do.'

'What?'

'I'll sell . . . the van . . . the ring . . . anything,' Murdo said. 'I'll give you the money and we'll call it quits.'

'What's going to happen then?' Rachel said.

'We'll go our separate ways,' Murdo said. 'I'll go back to the old man and the Benefits. You'll go back to the university, I suppose.'

'Murdo, when you were a wee boy, did you have a special toy you were fond of?' Rachel said.

'Yes,' Murdo said, 'I had a wee tractor my Uncle Duncan made out of a sardine tin.'

'What happened to it?'

'What happened to it?' Murdo said. 'What do you mean? One of the wheels got buckled and the whole thing fell apart.'

'Did you ever try to repair the wheel?' Rachel said.

'No.'

'You never learned how to repair things,' Rachel said. 'So, if a relationship between you and somebody else gets broken, you just skin out.'

'Are you talking about us?'

'Maybe.'

'Me and you, Rachel?' Murdo said. 'It'd never work out.'

'The Benbecula stud can't get it up any more?'

Murdo struggled to retain his dignity. 'Rachel,' he said, 'I'm going to do you a favour. I want you to be happy with me.'

'You get the money,' Rachel said, 'and I'll be happy.'

'I'll get it . . . the money I . . . uh, I got on loan,' Murdo said.

'You stole!' Rachel said. 'You went into my purse in Golspie and you stole a bundle of cash. That wasn't a loan!'

'No?'

'No,' Rachel said. 'You stole it! You could've asked.'

'I could've, if I'd been brave enough.'

'You bought drink with that "loan", didn't you?'

'Yes.'

'Do you like me?'

'I like you,' Murdo said.

'But in spite of that,' Rachel said, 'you turned your back on me and went for the drink.'

'Shut it,' Murdo said, 'I don't want to talk about drink.'

'I'm just asking, that's all,' Rachel said. 'Although I do say it myself, I know I'm attractive to men. But to you, Murdo, the drink was more attractive.'

'It wasn't as simple as that.'

'Wasn't it?'

'No,' Murdo said. 'You've got to understand, I had a good reason for going on the drink that night.'

'What good reason?' Rachel said.

'The tour was going to come to an end in a few days' time,' Murdo said. 'All during that day in Golspie, the feeling grew stronger and stronger within me that I was all alone in this world.'

'All alone?' Rachel said. 'But the place was jam packed that night.'

'Before we started,' Murdo said, 'I was at the door of the committee room peeping out at the people as they were coming in, and I wondered why I couldn't have a

29

life like them: a cosy little world where you'd be living with someone who loved you and whom you loved back, where you'd do your best, even though you'd never have glorious success.'

'And?' Rachel said.

'And I made myself a promise I'd be all right, and I took a dram,' Murdo said.

'And you got drunk?'

'Pissed as a newt,' Murdo said.

'And you carried on like that . . . in Dingwall and Aultbea . . .' Rachel said. 'Do you know that when you didn't appear in those places I still had to pay for the hall and I had to pay folk back for the tickets they'd bought?'

'I had no choice,' Murdo said.

'You're kidding yourself on, Murdo,' Rachel said.

'How?'

'You were frothing at the mouth just now telling me how you'd like to have a normal life like other people,' Rachel said. 'Lies! All your life, Murdo, you've been running away from the world by drinking too much. It's high time you stood up and showed us the real Murdo. The boozing is destroying you . . . and those nearest to you.'

'This is too hard,' Murdo said. 'I've got to go.'

'I can't stop you . . . and I can't help you either,' Rachel said.

'I know,' Murdo said. 'This one's up to me.'

'Murdo, people have been too willing to help you,' Rachel said. 'That's what's wrong. We're too fond of you, too fond of listening to you when you're on a creative roll, so you've been spoiled by us all. It was too easy for you to get forgiveness, and you got it too often.'

30

'I told you already I'd get you the money,' Murdo said.

'Let's have a proper deal,' Rachel said. 'You keep sober and get the money. Then I'll give you a reward.'

'A reward?'

'I'll give you the chance to make things better between us,' Rachel said.

'I'll keep off the drink, I'll get the money and . . . then, I'll get . . . the chance of getting close too you again?' Murdo said.

'I know you need some time to think about it,' Rachel said. 'It's just a proposal I'm making to you. I know what it's like to be alone.'

'I'll need to find someone with a fat wallet,' Murdo said.

'Go,' Rachel said. 'Remember, Murdo, two o'clock at the latest . . . and "the ocean of a thousand kisses" tonight.'

'How much did I borr— How much did I steal?' Murdo said.

'Three hundred pounds.'

'Well, I'll get us three hundred and fifty,' Murdo said and jumped out the van.

That's our Rachel. A tough lady. But she's not without fault herself. She used to smoke and I hated that. I told her it wasn't feminine. She chucked it and she now chews tobacco. Ha ha. Joking, only joking. But, she can be pretty determined when she puts her mind to it. When she wants to be, she can be as tough as . . . well, if you want proof of how tough she can be you don't have to look any further than her future career. She's going to be a lawyer. She's right, though. I've got to pull the pin on the bevvy. I've been going over the score. You don't believe me? You think I like looking like this? I've got heavier on the cigarettes as well. I'm trying to stop smoking. Which is a very hard thing to do. The other night, I did a very stupid thing. I fell asleep with a cigarette in my mouth. I could have set the whole house on fire. I was just lucky, I suppose. I was lying out in the garden path at the time . . . But getting back to the story – money, or lack of it – and me striving to be the man for Rachel that I have always failed to be. So far . . .

5

The housekeeper from Lewis

24 August 2010, 11.15 a.m.

Murdo walked straight into the Cocktail Bar of the Tartan Pagoda and took a seat on a bar stool facing Morag, vacuum-cleaner at the port. Morag was an ugly little woman in her seventies. She wore a striped overall and a large, hand-printed identity card that read 'HOUSEKEEPER'. Behind the extremely thick lenses of her spectacles were the mad eyes of a Presbyterian hysteric.

'Service? What do you mean you'll give me a servicing twice a year? I'm *Miss* MacIver, and I've never been called *Mistress*.'

'You're telling me you wouldn't fancy me coming over to tune your engine for you?'

'Bye, pervert!'

'The engine in the van.'

'What van?'

'The van I'm trying to sell you.'

'Don't be ridiculous, young man. What would I want a van for?'

'You could go to church in it on a Sunday.'

'May the Lord forgive you. I *walk* to church.'

'But maybe you know someone in your congregation who's looking for a van.'

'Quiet, young man, in case the Lord causes a judgement to be visited upon you. Nobody in our church believes in vans, or in cars or in lorries.'

'Willie the Tailor down our way thought the same as you. Poor man.'

'Who's Willie the Tailor and what happened to him?'

'A holy kind of chap from North Uist who came to a terrible end at Clachan church a year or two back.'

'How? What happened? What happened?'

'Well, the service was over about twelve o'clock, and he and a crowd of black Protestants were blethering outside the church right in the middle of the main road. Next thing they see is Calum MacCormack's lorry thundering flat out towards them. The others scattered but poor Willie stood there and said, "I don't believe in you". *Bang!* A wee bit too late. Archie MacPhee refused to box him . . . and the survivors are still going to counselling classes in Liniclate School.'

'Why are you getting rid of the van?'

'I need some money.'

'What did you do with the money you had?'

'I gave it away.'

'To whom?'

'To the Ethiopians. I saw a programme on the television last night where they were dying of starvation over there, and I felt sorry for them.'

'And you sent them the money straight away. Bless you. May you find your reward in heaven.'

'And I enclosed a wee note too.'

'What did you say in the letter?'

'I gave them some advice.'

36

'Advice?'

'Yes. I told them not to bother trying to plough or sow in the sand over there. Nothing grows in that soil.'

'What are they supposed to do?'

'They've got to go to where the food is. The best thing they can do is buy a ticket to Glasgow. That town is chock-a-block with McDonald's and Burger King and Pizza Hut. They must go on a plane to some place where there's plenty food.'

'I'd like to go on a plane too.'

'Where would you go?'

'I'd go anywhere. I'm sick to the teeth of Skye.'

Murdo glanced at his watch. 'Me too,' he said. ' "Early as I arose refreshed, One May morning in Os, Herds were lowing contentedly, As the sun gilded Leac an Stòir." '

'Oh, leave it out,' Morag said. 'In the summer here all I hear is the quacking of English tourists at Reception complaining, complaining about beds and about meals . . . and if I hear one more person asking for "a half of bitter", I swear, I'll take the poker off his skull . . .'

'Aren't you the Christian lady!'

'I wasn't reared on the Creamola in the Isle of Heather.'

'You're from Lewis, then?'

' "Shawbost is the most beautiful place, The place where I was brought up . . ." '

'Right.'

' "The eternal surge".'

'What?'

' "Without restraint without mercy pounding the sandy shore".'

'Oh, yes. Look, I was thinking . . .'

'But you're from South Uist, aren't you?'

'From Benbecula actually – Kyles Flodda, but when I sleep in for good I'll be buried in Nunton. You know, "the township of the old women"?'

'Who were these old women?'

'Nuns.'

'You're, er, a Pa— You're a Catholic, then?'

'That's what I am, darling. I almost went into the priesthood after I left school, but the Catholic Church rejected me.'

'Why?'

'I preferred young girls to young boys.' Murdo spread his arms, palms outward, and raised his shoulders in a gesture of apology. 'Hey, I'm just winding you up. Sorry.'

'Do you go to confession?'

'I used to go.'

'Oh, I'd love to go to confession. I've got so much to tell.'

'Really?'

'Can you take food in with you . . . maybe a blanket and a wee pillow?'

'Well . . .'

'I'd love to get the chance to do that.'

'What?'

'To open up to someone without considering what they thought of me.'

'You're right,' Murdo said. 'It must be great to be able to speak to someone you trust about the little worries that grind you down.'

'That's what's wrong with folk today. They're drowning in their own thought. They won't share with other people. So, they don't really know who they are. I'll bet you don't know who you are either.'

'Uh-huh, I can't deny it.'

'Pedro Gonzalez. "There is a Pedro Gonzalez for everyone, an adequate man, but beneath age and clothing, he has no name . . ."' the housekeeper intoned breathlessly.

'I didn't know any of the Gonzalez family. All I heard was that they came from Garryhilly or somewhere like that up in south Uist.'

'Pablo Neruda, a famous poet from Chile, wrote that, you clown.'

'Oh, it was the Peterannas from Daliburgh – Uist Builders – I was thinking about,' Murdo said.

Morag spoke apologetically. 'I'm one of these people who just love to read.'

'I'm not. Torlum was the school I went to. In Donald Macleod's wee blue bus.'

'Most of the time it's the Bible I read.'

'I hate interrupting you but . . .'

'First Letter to the Corinthians, Chapter Nine, Verse Seven. "It is better to marry than to burn."'

'Uh . . . I wanted to talk to you . . . about . . .'

'Fortunately, I won't burn, though I never did get married.'

'But you did have a boyfriend at one time, though?'

'Oh, yes. But I gave him the elbow.'

'Why?'

'I caught him in bed with the woman next door.'

'You must have been hurt to the quick.'

'No, I was just grateful he'd broken up with the helicopter pilot!'

'Nice one,' Murdo said.

'I think it's about time you got married,' Morag said, 'before you burn.'

'Who to?'

'The one you really love with all your heart. You know yourself who she is.'

'Aw, you know what marriages in the islands are like,' Murdo said, affecting a deep growl. '"Mary, pet, I'm pretty fond of you."' He smacked the palm of his left hand with the back of his right, as though delivering a slap to someone. '"And don't you ever forget it!"' Murdo laughed nervously. Morag didn't.

'Don't move,' Morag screamed. 'Keep away from me.'

'Whoa, lady! I'm not going to touch you.'

'Make one move, and you'll get a punch from me that'll level you.'

'Wait a minute . . . All I need is . . .'

'I know what you need.'

'You do?'

'Sure.'

'So, you know that I'm short of money, don't you?'

'Is that all?' She paused. 'Tell me what you really want.'

'I've told you before. I want to sell something.'

'Everybody wants to sell something,' Morag said.

'I'm not like that. Come here, I've got collateral.'

'What kind of disease is that?'

'My van. Come over here to the window till you see it.'

'I'm not moving.'

'Wait, we've got off on the wrong foot here.'

'I suppose you're just like that other fellow who works in television – that man in Room 3,' Morag said.

'No! All I want from you is for you to tell me who's carrying cash around this place.'

'Cash?'

'That's it.'

'You're not going to rape me?'

'No, indeed I'm not.'

'I didn't think so. I recognised you had a full heart.'

'A full heart . . . and an empty wallet.'

'As soon as I saw you I knew that you were born to love. That you were ruled by the desires of the flesh.'

'Forget the desires of the flesh,' Murdo said. 'Look, I've got to be out of this hotel by twelve o'clock. Let's talk about money. Can we?'

'Okay,' Morag said. She slowly moved to the gantry and poured herself a large drink. She turned towards the motionless Murdo. 'Fancy a glass?'

'No, thanks.'

There was a slight pause before Morag spoke again. 'Are you going on the Lochmaddy ferry?'

'If I make it onto the boat, I'm going to Tarbert, and then on to Stornoway . . . maybe.'

'Stornoway! Oh, dry my perspiration! My favourite town in all the world!'

'Really?'

'"On a misty evening I was on the street in Stornoway . . ."'

'If I don't get a bed, I'll end up on the street myself.'

'The town that never sleeps . . .'

'Who could sleep in Stornoway with all these freaks and weirdos wandering around The Narrows every night?'

'Great Stornoway with its castle.'

'Look, can I ask . . .?'

'Do you know this? I have dreams about the town of Stornoway.'

'You don't say.'

'The nearer you are to Stornoway, the nearer you are to the Lord.'

'I don't know. I spent two years there . . . one night.'

'Have you been there right enough?'

'Many times.'

'Oh, how lucky you are!'

'I go over there on business now and again.'

'What kind of work do you do?'

Murdo paused before answering. 'I'm an actor.'

'Goodness! One of the guests in the hotel is in the same business.'

'He may be. I don't know him in any case . . . Can we . . .?'

'The pair of you will have a great deal in common.'

'I doubt it.'

'I'll need to try and get the pair of you together.'

'Don't bother.' Murdo said. 'Whenever I meet a half-wit, I'm as sick as a dog.'

6

Murdo pricks up his ears

24 August 2010, 11.30 a.m.

'You'll get on well together,' Morag said. 'His company's called Etive Television. He seems to have a lot of money.'

'I'd rather mutilate myself than meet with someone like . . . What did you say?'

'What about?'

'About money.'

'He gives the impression he's not short of a bob or two.'

'How do you know?'

'He made Mr Barrington-Smythe an offer for this place. Barrington-Smythe and his wife – if that's what you call her – they wanted a hundred and fifty thousand for it. The man from Etive Television would only give seventy thousand. I just hate it when people haggle over prices. It's not polite, is it?'

'Er, well, no.' Murdo paused. 'Tell me more about Barrington-Smythe and his wife.'

'He's as mad as a hatter. Into pottery. He makes mugs out of clay . . . and statues.'

'What kind of statues?'

'Two kinds.'

'Who does he model them on?'

'Jesus Christ and Frank Bruno.'

'Is there some connection between them?'

'They're almost identical in every respect.'

'Jesus and Frank Bruno?'

'Our Saviour is as black as pitch with beads of sweat all over his body. Thick lips and large nostrils. All he's wearing is a pair of shorts.'

'Jesus has become a boxer?'

'Oh, no. The only difference between them is that our Lord doesn't wear boxing gloves. Frank Bruno does.'

'Okay. Barrington-Smythe doesn't have both oars in the water. Does his . . . the live-in have a bank book?'

'Och, Barrington-Smythe ordered her from a J.D. Williams catalogue,' Morag said. 'Just as soon as they sell the hotel, she'll take her whack and before you can say "Missing you already" that'll be her off on a plane to Bangkok or Barra. No, sorry, she'd be stoned to death in Barra. She'll head for the Far East. She's obsessed with anything from China.'

'Things don't look too promising.'

'Don't say that, son. There is one who will come to your aid.'

'If it's a black man wearing boxing shorts, I'm not in the slightest bit interested.'

'What a numpty you are! The man from Etive Television.'

'I don't want to hear another word about him.'

'You're asking me about people who'd maybe buy your van, and I'm telling you that the man from Etive Television has got money.'

'I don't know . . .'

'Irrespective of the value of the thing, he'll only give you half of that. That man would go to He— He'd go to the Devil himself for a bargain . . . on wheels!'

Murdo was silent for a couple of seconds. 'Hmmm.'

'Go and have a word with him. He's in Room 3.'

Murdo produced a pen and notebook with a flourish. 'Wait a second, wait till I get something down on paper.'

'Do you write as well?'

'Oh, yes . . . You know, little sketches . . . and stuff like that. Torlum was the school I went to.'

'In Donald Macleod's wee blue bus.' Morag sniffed. 'I have to go. I've got real work to do.'

Murdo scribbled furiously. 'Go, go. I've got about half an hour left to get this down on paper . . . so that I'll maybe save my life.'

'If you were a good Christian, you'd understand that He alone can raise you on high.'

'That's a thing I always wondered about with Christians,' Murdo said.

'What?'

'Why they had to keep going back to church every week.'

'What's wrong with that?'

'Are they retarded or what? What goes on inside their heads? How does it go again? Jesus . . . good . . . Satan . . . bad? Maybe it's the other way round. Jesus . . . bad . . .? Och, I can't remember. I'll go back to the church next week and I'll listen real carefully.'

'How dare you speak like that!' Morag said.

'I'm sorry if I offended you, but it's just that I'm excited.'

'You're excited?'

'Yes. The muse is sitting on my shoulder.'

'What's your muse saying to you?'

'Go get him, tiger!'

There was a slight delay before Morag said, 'I've got the toilet to clean.'

'If you could leave me alone for a wee while, that would suit me.'

'I'm off,' Morag said.

'I'm truly grateful to you. You've just given me tremendous encouragement.' Murdo continued to write up a storm.

'Look, I hope nobody's going to get into trouble through me,' Morag said.

'You won't, for sure, darling. Maybe trouble's brewing, but not for you.'

'That's good. Every man for himself and God for everyone. Isn't that it?' Morag walked over to a mirror, hooked her fingers in the corners of her mouth and stretched her cheeks out wide to examine her teeth. 'Is my hair looking okay? I'm going upstairs now to do Mr Etive Television's room. He's such a nice man. As kind as a seagull.'

'What do you mean?'

'He's always giving folk presents.'

'Like what?'

'Yesterday he gave me a photograph of Calum Kennedy signed by his own fair hand.'

'That was a present?'

'He even showed me a picture of his girlfriend.'

'He's married, is he?'

'Not yet.'

'Who's he marrying?'

'May the Lord forgive me for mocking His work – but she's *really* ugly. If Moses had known about her there

46

would have been one more commandment! Still, he's thinking of getting engaged.'

Murdo stopped writing and looked at her. He carefully laid his pen down and thrust his hand into his trouser pocket then, reassured, picked up his pen again. 'He hasn't proposed to her yet, has he?'

'He's going to when they discharge her from the asylum and when she comes off the lithium. She had a nervous breakdown about eighteen months ago.'

'She's barking mad?'

'Well, yes, but her people are rotten with money.'

'Your man's going to marry her for the sake of her money?'

'How should I know why he's marrying her. But there's definitely going to be a wedding . . . just as soon as she reaches her sixtieth birthday.'

'He'd prefer his women to be young, beautiful and intelligent, but he'll take an old boiler who's off her head, just so long as she's well off?'

'I don't know about that. All I know is, they're going to get engaged. I heard them talking about it.'

'Who was talking?'

'Himself and . . . you know . . . her.'

'The loony? God be round about me, is there another psycho in the place?'

'Do you know what, young man? You ask too many questions. You didn't give a fig about that poor soul upstairs while back. Now you can't stop interrogating me about him.'

'I'm just trying to understand what's going on in the life of a poor unfortunate who's in the same racket as me.'

'Well, Sam, that's the man from Etive Television . . .'

'I know, I know.'

'Well, Sam and . . . the woman of the house were talking and . . .'

'You were listening.'

'Yes. And I heard about the two-step deal.'

'What?'

'The two-step deal.'

'What the hell's the two-step deal?'

'First of all, Sam will give them five per cent of the offering price to them. That's three thousand five hundred pounds.'

'And?'

'They'll have the espousals before the banns here, in the Tartan Pagoda, hundreds of toffs from all over, and we'll have them for at least a fortnight, and if everything goes off all right and if the batty old bride is happy with the celebrations . . .'

'What happens then?'

'Maybe he'll buy the place – as a base for his company, you understand? – and give our old man the rest of the money.'

'That's the two-step deal, is it?'

'Yes.'

'You could do with four eyes in your head if you're going to be dealing with the bold Sam,' Murdo said.

'Oh, he's certainly a smart cookie.'

'Do you know if Barrington-Smythe's agreed to this yet?'

'It's none of my business. And it's none of your business either.'

Murdo patted an object in his pocket. 'Has he bought a ring yet?'

'What?'

'DOES HE HAVE A RING TO GIVE TO THE HALF-WIT?'

'Do you know this? I don't know who's the craziest in this place. You're blasting my ears like a rutting stag. Manners, man, manners.'

'I'm sorry.'

Morag went behind the bar counter and poured a generous drink for herself. 'I know that you're excited,' she said, 'what with all that talk about getting married and about love.' She turned to face him with an understanding smile. 'Will you take a drink?'

'No, no, I don't drink any more. I'm high on life. From now on, I don't want to escape from it any more. My mind needs to be clear. A glorious future awaits me.'

'A glorious future?'

'Wonderful! Money. Love . . . Rachel.'

'Who's Rachel?'

'She whose curling hair flows down in ringlets, like the strings on the fiddle, over her two shoulders.'

'Well, maybe Mr Etive Television's girlfriend isn't quite like that, but he wants to marry her anyway.'

'I want a woman to handle and to hold . . . to love and not love her . . . I want to feel her teeth in my kisses.'

'I suppose that's the way Mr Kerr is feeling too.'

'Does the man have that amount of money? I mean, over three thousand pounds?'

'I haven't seen it . . . yet. I'm not a snoop. I'm a communicant.'

'Do you think they'll sell the hotel under these terms?'

'He'd sell it for a lump of clay. I'm not so sure about her. She used to be one of those hippies.'

'What was she?'

'She smokes . . . er, that gear.'

49

'And that means she'd sell the place to the first person who'd offer her cash?'

'No. She's from Harris, although she was brought up abroad. And you know how light-headed they can be.'

'I can't make head nor tail of this.'

'She has no religion. Well, she has a sort of religion. She talks to the spirit that resides within her body.'

'It's acid rain from Chernobyl that's caused this.'

'As far as I am concerned, I don't care who owns the place. But, to tell the truth, I'd be delighted to welcome the man who put *Our Land* on our screens.'

'Did you enjoy it?'

'It was splendid, wasn't it?'

'Pass the bucket. I'm going to be sick.'

Morag passed him the bucket. 'Gracious me! Here! Go into the toilet!'

Murdo shook his head in amusement. 'Look,' he said, 'I cannot thank you enough for all your help today. I'm deeply indebted to you.'

'You are?'

'Now, if you'll excuse me, I've really got to finish this script.' Murdo turned his back on her and resumed his writing. He looked up as Morag gathered her cleaning materials and prepared to leave. 'May my god give his blessing' he intoned, 'as I hatch this lying story, a story that will get me out of this fix and deliver my beautiful girl to me.' He checked his watch. 'Shit, nearly twelve o'clock already. Light of my life, the unrest of my spirit will depart when the skull and brains of Mr Etive Television go in splatters.'

'Cheerie,' Morag said.

7

A secret meeting in Room 3

24 August 2010, 11.45 p.m.

Sam was sitting on the bed surveying a dozen or so cases. He looked at his watch, picked up a brown leather case. He opened it and with evident pleasure viewed the contents.

Morag shuffled into the room. 'Mr . . . er, Mr Etive Television? Sorry to bother you. Can I tidy your room for you?'

'What are you doing here? You were going to send a fax to your boss, right?'

'Fax?' Morag said. 'I wouldn't know a fax from the leg of a cow. I just wanted to clean your room.'

'Uh, who told you that Sam Kerr's accounts were up here?'

'Nobody! I'm the housekeeper!'

'Mmmm . . . Sam Kerr has many enemies. When you're King of the Castle in the world of Gaelic television, there are a lot of people who want to sling you on to the rubbish tip.'

Morag moved towards the bed. 'Well, I'd better get on with cleaning this tip up. I'll just put your briefcase . . .'

'DON'T YOU DARE TOUCH THAT BRIEF-
CASE! HAND IT OVER!'

'I just want to . . .'

'GIVE ME THAT BRIEFCASE!'

Morag clasped the briefcase against her bosom.
'Won't you let me help you?'

'LET GO THAT BRIEF—'

Sam grabbed the briefcase. As he grunted and Morag
squeaked a tug-of-war ensued. The unlocked briefcase
opened and was dropped. Bundles of banknotes cas-
caded to the floor.

'Goodness me!' Morag said. 'Where did all this
money come from?'

Sam screamed, 'FROM EVERY OUNCE OF
FLESH, OF BLOOD, OF BONE AND MARROW
IN MY BODY!'

'Now, don't get excited,' Morag said. 'I'll help you.'

'When you . . . almost kill yourself . . . making
programmes like *Our Land* . . . you're worth every
penny.'

'*Our Land* . . . *Our Land* . . . Oh, Mr Kerr, I can't tell
you how much I enjoyed that programme! Our own
ancestors . . . people without flaw or blemish . . .
deceived by greedy men . . .'

Sam looked at her and realised he had a real fan before
him. 'Mmmm . . . maybe you're not telling lies.'

'No! I swear I'm not telling lies!'

'Well, in that case, maybe you can help. I'll give you a
contract. How would you fancy four hundred pounds at
the end of every month?'

'Oh, bless you, son! Yes, I'll help you all you need! I'll
put all this stuff away first.' Morag quickly packed the
money in the case.

Sam looked at her approvingly. 'That's more like it.' He arranged himself on the bed in languid pose, watching as Morag closed the case. She deposited it by his side. He wriggled over to the end of the bed, taking the case with him. He patted the vacant space with the palm of his hand. 'Come here,' he said. 'I want to talk to you.'

Morag didn't hesitate. She scooted over to the bed and listened attentively.

'You know I'm about to be married, don't you?' Sam said.

'That's right.'

'And you know that we intend to have the espousals in the Tartan Pagoda?'

'Oh, I was so pleased to hear that!'

'Well, if that's to happen, I need you to help me.'

'Me?'

'I want to buy the hotel.'

'If . . . if you do buy it, you'll never get an employee as loyal as me.'

Suki's voice was heard from outside. 'Morag?'

'Who's that?' Sam said.

'The Bitch! Suki!' Morag hissed.

'Listen, I've got a proposition for you.'

'She's always creeping about . . . guarding that furniture of hers that's supposed to be so precious.'

'Does she ever leave the place?'

'Very rarely. She can turn up anywhere.'

'And Nigel . . . the husband?'

Suki's voice was heard again. 'Where are you, Morag?'

'Coming!' Morag called. Then she turned to Sam. 'We don't see very much of Nigel.'

'Why's that?'

'Oh, he's an artist. He's involved with "creative work", as she calls it.'

Sam opened the briefcase and allowed Morag to look at the entire cache of money for fully five seconds. 'I have a great interest in art too. I prefer pictures – pictures of the Queen.'

'Aren't they gorgeous!'

Suki shouted again, 'Hurry up, Morag. Nigel will be starving.'

Morag said under her breath, 'Let him eat hay.' She turned to Sam. 'I've never seen anything as beautiful as this ever.'

'Do you think the artist would like to cast an eye on my picture collection?'

'How much money have you got there?'

'Three and a half grand.'

'Nigel's never seen that amount of money in the one place before.'

'I'd like to meet up with Nigel.'

'He'll be in the studio all day.'

'Can I pay him a little visit?'

'You won't get in. She locks him in first thing every morning.'

'She locks him in?'

'I can get the key.'

'When?'

'After two o'clock.'

Sam stared at Morag intently . . . very intently. He smiled. 'I've never been in a situation like this before, but my interest has been piqued by what you've told me . . .' He turned and walked quickly over to the bedside table. He punched random numbers into his useless mobile. 'Excuse me. This phone call I'm about to make, it's the call that's going to change your life.'

'Ooooh!'

Sam pretended to make a phone call. 'Hi, Amanda? . . . Sam Kerr here . . . I crave a favour . . . This very minute, arrange a short vacation for a lady I've just met here . . . Yeah, send her the tickets right away . . . Write this down: THE LITTLE UGLY OLD WOMAN . . . HOUSEKEEPER . . . TARTAN PAGODA HOTEL . . . UIG . . . ISLE OF SKYE . . . *Ciao!*'

Sam smiled broadly. 'Congratulations, darling! You've won the prize! A weekend in Stornoway . . .'

'Stornoway? Ooooh!'

Sam continued, '. . . accompanied by the Free Church minister . . . of your own choice!'

'Oh, thank you, Mr Kerr!'

'You can take these camera cases downstairs when you've finished in here. I must have a bite of lunch.'

'Whatever you say, Mr Kerr.' Morag remained motionless, staring enquiringly at Sam.

'Is there anything bothering you?' Sam said.

'Will I see you again?'

'No. I'm filming in Ha— in South Uist all this week and then I'm off to . . . er, Africa . . . uh, South Africa.'

'Er . . .'

'What's wrong? Have you told me everything?'

'Oh, yes! I was just wondering, who's going to pay me?'

'Pay you? Oh, yeah. Your retainer, you mean? Well, I'll tell you what I'll do . . . First of all . . . don't you worry . . . what do you call it? . . . I'll phone our Contract Department in Edinburgh and they'll write to you and tell you what duties you'll have to perform in return for your monthly cheque.'

'But the money . . . the money, man,' Morag insisted.

'What about it? Is it not enough for you?'

'You don't understand. How do I get my hands on it?'

'Oh, it's Big Patrick – the Eriskay Giant – that'll hand it over.'

'The Eriskay Giant?'

'He'll approach you and he'll give you an envelope . . . just as soon as you say the blessed words.'

'The blessed words?'

' "A good thing's worth waiting for",' Sam said.

' "A good thing's worth waiting for"? That's what I've got to say before I get the money?'

'That's it.'

'When will he come?'

Sam glanced at his watch. 'I wouldn't be a bit surprised if he came . . . I don't know . . . maybe even today . . . or tomorrow.'

'Terrific, Mr Kerr. Whatever you say, Mr Kerr. I can't tell you how sorry I am about our wrestling match . . . but I'm glad . . . I mean . . . everything worked out all right for us in the end.'

Sam moved across to the doorway. He turned and spoke to her seriously, 'Not a word to anyone about what you've heard here . . . or what you've seen either . . . You're a member of the television community now. Know what I mean? "Slippery is the threshold of the big house." '

8

East and West

Rachel was standing in the reception area when Sam swaggered in. Suki, well-preserved, late thirties, wearing a sarong, long black hair tied back with a piece of multi-coloured ribbon, was standing behind a desk upon which were a brass bell and a telephone. Next to the phone was a wooden box with a slot for coins on the top. The words TELEPHONE CALLS were stencilled on the front.

'Ah, light of my life,' Sam said, 'whaddya say?'

Suki stared balefully right through him.

'What a splendid place this is for a wedding celebration!' Sam gushed.

Suki turned her back on him and pretended to busy herself with some paperwork.

'Just as soon as you sign these papers, I'm going to rename this place "Tartan Pagoda Productions". Neat, eh?'

'Uh-huh,' Suki grunted, 'but you'll never get my name on any paper.'

'How's that?'

'Place belongs to Nigel. Nothing to do with me.'

'Oh. Yeah.'

'If it were up to me, I wouldn't part with it at your price. And I certainly wouldn't sell it to you.'

'Why not?'

'You're the guy who ravaged Gaelic television programmes single-handed with *Our Land*.'

'I got seven awards for *Our Land* at the Celtic Film and Television Festival in Stenhousemuir.'

'You should have got seven years.'

'What didn't you like about the programme?'

'Everything. You're the one who introduced all the rotten things that have sickened Gaelic-speakers.'

'What rotten things?'

'Lowland people without a word of Gaelic trying to speak the language.' Suki did a take-off of a monoglot English speaker attempting to read an autocue. ' "Ka kritch mee nak ale an t-àm akin toshakag." Americans and English folk telling us about Highland history.' She affected an American and a Southern English accent. ' "Yeah, my people were Scotch-Irish – from right on the border!" "Communities where an oral tradition predominates is so much out of the experience of the modern Western world that it is extremely difficult for anyone without first-hand knowledge to imagine how a language can be cultivated without being written to any extent, or what oral history is like, or how it is propagated and added to from generation to generation. The consciousness of the Gaelic mind may be described as possessing historical continuity and religious sense; it may be said to exist in a vertical plane. The consciousness of the modern Western world, on the other hand, may be said to exist in a horizontal plane, possessing breadth and extent, dominated by a scientific materialism and a concern with purely contemporary happenings.

There is a profound difference between the two mental attitudes, which represent the different spirits of different ages, and are very much in conflict." What shite!'

'Wow! You've certainly devoted a lot of thought to this.'

'Do you know what worries me most about this legacy of yours?'

'No, but I've a feeling you're going to tell me anyway.'

'Just as there are people still alive throughout Europe who laboured mightily to establish the Third Reich, so there are people living down in Glasgow who saw *Our Land* and, worse still, made this programme. They are in our midst. They are biding their time. They will rise again.'

'Isn't that funny? I've just received a commission to make another historical series, *Children of the Exiles*.'

'Oh, for God's sake!'

'That's why I need an address in the Highlands . . . Listen, where is Nigel?'

'In the studio.'

'Can I talk to him?'

'No, not unless I'm there.'

'Oh, I see. Listen to me,' Sam said as he began to become angry. 'This hotel is going down the tubes. How many people were in the house last night? Four! Me, my PA and a walking sponge from Benbecula and his bird . . .'

Suki retreated to the office door where she stared at Sam with disgust.

'Where did that babe go anyway?' Sam said. 'Quite tidy, she was. I wouldn't mind giving her an audition . . . yuk-yuk.'

Rachel moved forward to the counter, studiously

ignoring Sam, indicated to Suki that she wished to use the phone and extracted some coins and a few banknotes from her purse. She put some coins into the box, picked up the phone and dialled.

'Hello, Daddy? Is Mummy there? . . . Okay, Uig in Skye . . . We're . . . I'm in a hotel . . . No. Well, yes, he is . . . until two o'clock anyway . . . I'll maybe stay here for another night . . . it depends on what happens . . .'

Sam, obviously reminded of something, pulled out a mobile phone and rapidly punched some buttons. He slammed the mobile against the counter. 'Bloody phones . . . shit . . . piece of shit . . . DAMN IT!'

Rachel continued to speak to her father. 'I'm sorry, Dad, a gentleman here has just lost it completely . . . Tell Mummy . . .'

Sam plucked the receiver from Rachel's hand and pushed her aside with a sweeping movement of his other hand.

Rachel shouted, 'THERE'S A CHANCE THERE'S GOING TO BE AN ADDITION TO THE FAMILY!'

Sam slammed the receiver down, picked it up and rapidly dialled another number. Teeth bared, he talked rapidly. 'Hi, Charlie, this is your main man talking, making hay, making your pimples go away . . . Don't interrupt . . . All rested up? 'Cause have we got visions to mix or awards to win? . . . Look, Charlie, there's nothing wrong with Mrs Mackenzie's council house. As I was saying . . . Because, see, this job we're in, the money's great, right? . . . Vanessa's network, we're regional . . . Money's great, because we work hard. And there's plenty of work for you guys. Charlie, cameras are downstairs. Tell Linda to phone HQ and inform D.A. the mobiles don't work up here. Tell Bill to pick up the tickets for the van and crew, and make sure you park in the right lane . . . That's right, Tarbert . . . Hope you put the cones out for the Range Rover. I'll meet you there . . . Wait, I've got to weigh the hotel in first and have a bite of lunch. Correction: I'm having lunch, then I'll pay the bill . . . That's it, Charlie. Never give a sucker an even break. Ha ha! Look this call is costing the company a fortune, I'll meet you at the Range Rover in an hour's time, my man . . . *Ciao!*'

Rachel stepped forward. 'Excuse me.'

'Charlie, you still there? . . . Can I bum a packet of cigarettes off you? Mine are, uh, still in the shop. Ha ha! Still in the shop . . . Right away, of course. *Ciao!*'

'I was using the phone,' Rachel said.

Sam dialled another number, oblivious. 'Yeah, Donald Allan? Yeah, Sam Kerr here . . . Okay. Well, actually, it's not too bad at all. The mobiles don't work, though . . . Oh, did she? Well, the evening meal wasn't all that bad . . . No, the owner's English, married to a Chinese chick or something . . . That's right, Donald Allan, the cooking's kind of what you'd expect a guy from England and a bird from Hong Kong to come up with . . . Yeah, you eat and an hour later you're starving . . . and you also have an uncontrollable urge to open a pottery in the Highlands. Ha ha! . . . The two-step deal? . . . Like a good Gaelic song . . . Oh, they'll sell sure as anything . . . I've got the wife wrapped around my little finger already!'

Suki opened the office door and stood motionless.

Sam stared at her. 'Uh . . . I've got to go . . . Oh, geez . . .' He replaced the phone and smiled nervously at Suki who proffered an invoice. He looked blankly down at the paper, slowly took out a chequebook and in embarrassed silence wrote out a cheque.

Suki affected a cod Chinese accent. 'Coffee? How many? One? Two?'

Sam grabbed the invoice and made a halting run to the door. He used similar telegraphese. 'No, no coffee. Big hurry . . . I . . . uh, me. Visions to mix . . . Oh, geez! So, uh, chop–chop, uh . . . Oh, geez!'

'Pssst!'

Sam looked at her.

Suki was brandishing a hideous statue of a black man wearing boxing gloves. 'Me give you gnome. You give me money.'

'No!'

'You sure you don't want buy gnome? Is no' clear to me why no' buy gnome.'

Sam mumbled, 'If your eyes weren't as squint as a Chinaman's, it would be clear to you. I've never seen anything so ugly in all my life.'

Suki pointed to the clock on the wall in the ten past twelve position. 'Look at clock.'

'What about it?'

'It's stopped.'

'And?'

'You make clock stop. Yo' face so very ugly. Poor clock give up ghost. Now he stopped.'

Sam departed in the huff. Rachel doubled up with laughter.

9

Girl talk

Suki spoke in a strong Harris accent. 'If it's a crime for me to sell twenty Regal tipped to a lad who's under sixteen years of age, why isn't it a crime for that arsehole to be on the streets without supervision?'

'I don't . . . I don't know. Oh, did you see his face?' Rachel composed herself. 'Rachel MacKinnon, Room 5.'

'Room 5. Weren't there two of you?'

'Yes, at first . . . but he slept in the van.'

'A rude, fat butterball, very drunk . . . Is that the one?'

'That's Murdo.'

'He's the guy who hit on me in the bar last night, swaggering like John Wayne, and asked me a question.' She lowered her voice and spoke in a nasal drawl. '"Hey, honey, can I buy you . . . a tractor?"'

'That's the kind of thing he'd say when he's drunk.'

'Tell him not to wear that jacket if he ever comes in here during the day.'

'Why?'

'The young guys'll cut it up and smoke it.' Suki consulted a book. 'Ah, you're leaving us today, is that right?'

63

'Well, I wanted to talk to you about that . . . That is, if you've got a minute.'

'It would be a pleasure, young woman.' Suki placed her elbows on the counter and leaned forward in conspiratorial fashion. 'Since I've got shot of Sam the Scam, there's nothing I'd like better than a little chat with someone like yourself.'

'Sam the –'

'An arrogant braggart. He's made the odd programme for the Beeb. They're all crap. He's also terribly mean. He'd steal the worm from a blind hen.'

'What a despicable miser!'

'That's the word we're looking for. He wants to buy this place. But he's constantly cutting the price. My biggest fear is that he'll get to Nigel – that's my husband – and he'll be tempted by a very large sum of ready cash.' She looked at Rachel seriously. 'What did you want to talk about, Rachel?'

'Uh, well, I, I was looking for some . . . advice. I mean . . .'

'Advice! You've come to the right place, haven't you? All the wisdom of the East just pours out of me.'

'Was it from China this wisdom came?'

'Kyles Scalpay. That's where my granny on my father's side came from. "Shanghai's Wife" she was known as. My grandfather was a river pilot in Shanghai once upon a time and he was the one who brought all this furniture home.'

'Well, I thought . . . I mean . . .'

'That I had more than a drop of Chinese blood in me? No, though my skin is a tad yellow, but there's folk on Scott Road far darker than me. No, I'm as Heilan' as peat. Oh, I like to have the things my grandfather

64

collected round about me. The Tartan Pagoda is a kind of shrine to my granny.'

'Oh, I get it.'

'But what are you going to do about Murdo?'

'I don't know. I've given him an ultimatum: unless he comes up with money, I'm off on the ferry this afternoon and I'm leaving him here.'

'Good decision, Rachel. That'll keep him on his toes . . . that is, if he's really fond of you.' She paused for a moment. 'So, what's all this talk of yours about money?'

'It's . . . it's to do with Murdo as well.'

'Everything seems to revolve around him.'

'Yeah, it does, doesn't it?'

'Now,' Suki said, 'shall I make up your bill?'

'As the old guy from Barra said, "I'm in a quadrangle".'

'Won't you tell me?'

'I can pay for last night's lodgings and still have just enough to get home, or I can stay another night – with Murdo.'

'Give me both hands, Rachel.' Suki held Rachel's hands lightly.

'What is it we're doing?' Rachel said.

'Let us pray.'

Rachel rapidly took her hands away. 'Uh, I don't think so, if it's all the same to you.'

'Don't be silly. You're not going to be praying to the Lord God Almighty. You're just going to be putting some questions to yourself.'

'No,' Rachel said. 'Look, I don't want to hurt your feelings. It's a matter of indifference to me what religion other people believe in, just so long as they don't try to put iron horseshoes on my feet.'

'You're not listening to me, Rachel.' Suki seized Rachel's hands in her own once more. 'All I'm trying to do is teach you how you can have a conversation between yourself and the Rachel that's deep inside you.'

'So that I can talk to myself?'

'That's it,' Suki said. 'So that you can draw upon the huge amount of power and love you hold inside.'

'God be round about me! If I start talking to myself in public, guys will be on the phone saying "Check all mental hospitals for empty beds"!'

'Have you heard of yin and yang?' Suki said.

'No. I'd hazard a guess they had something to do with pornography.'

'Yang is like fire. If the fire is too hot, you'll burn the cabbage. Yin is like water. If you have too much water in the pot, the cabbage will rot.'

Rachel stared at her in horror. 'You've already turned my head into broth, lady.'

'Do you trust me enough to do as I tell you – with the result that you'll change your life forever?'

There was a short pause. Finally Rachel said, 'Okay. What do I have to do?'

'Firstly, close your eyes.'

Rachel closed her eyes. 'What now?'

'Allow your mind to drift with the wind . . . slowly, flowingly . . . just as the morning dew departs from the greensward at sunrise . . .'

'Mmmm.'

'Repeat after me: Where would you have me go?'

'Where would you have me go?'

After a brief pause, Suki spoke again. 'What would you have me do?'

'What would you have me do?'

A second or two went by.

'What would you have me say, and to whom?'

'What would you have me say, and to whom?'

There was a long delay. Suki released her grip and looked expectantly at Rachel. 'Well?'

'Well, what?'

'Are you going or are you staying?'

'I'll stay another night – if the room's still vacant.'

'You're more than welcome,' Suki said. 'I won't charge you for the room tonight. Just give me twelve pounds.'

'Thank you. That's terrific.'

'Come on, aren't you formal, young lady! You can be informal with me. Just call me Suki. That's my correct name anyway . . . Suki Morrison.' Suki looked closely at Rachel. 'What are you going to do about him?'

'That's up to him. If he gets the money . . .'

'What'll the pair of you do?'

'Well . . . I suppose we'll have a night of mad, passionate love.'

'I hope he makes it.'

'Me too,' Rachel said.

'Not for his sake, but for yours . . .'

'But if he doesn't get what he owes me, and if he doesn't stay sober . . . well, he'll be sitting on the chair all night with his legs crossed.'

'If it's your destiny to sleep with him tonight, ask your heart what you ought to do.' Suki paused. 'What size are you?'

'Pardon?'

'What size do you take in clothes?'

'Ten. Why?'

'Couldn't be better,' Suki said. 'You'll knock everybody out with the cheongsam.'

'What are you talking about?'

'Wear the beautiful silk dress I've got for you and every man in the place will have the hots for you.' She paused. 'Including Murdo.'

'What if he's not seduced by the dress?'

'Find somebody who will be.'

'Hey, Suki,' Rachel said, 'I'm very fond of Murdo. I don't want anyone else.'

'If you look nice for him, well, you'll be doing him a favour. Listen, I don't care if it works out between you and Murdo or not. Either you'll sleep with him or you'll not. All I want is to see you in that Chinese dress.'

'Then I'll ask you just one question,' Rachel said.

'Go ahead.'

'Why are you so keen on me putting on this dress?'

Suki brandished a statue of the boxer/Saviour. 'Look, I'm married to a dunderhead who doesn't know the difference between Frank Bruno and our Saviour. Amn't I entitled to a little romance?'

Both women broke into laughter.

'Okay,' Rachel said, 'but we'll have to be quick.'

'What's your hurry?'

'I want to find out how Murdo got on.'

They parted. Suki went into the office. Rachel ran upstairs with her bags.

10

Rehearsal

24 August 2010, 12.30 p.m.

Murdo was crouched by the bed, methodically going through suitcases and trunks, discarding wigs, dresses, Highland dress, Wellington boots etc. – all the props needed by a two-handed theatrical company on tour. When he had finished selecting items of clothing he went into his trouser pocket and slowly and carefully took out the small jewellery box. 'Oh, ya beauty!' he said.

He closed the box, reverently almost, and placed it in the inside pocket of a beat-up old jacket. Quickly Murdo moved to a pre-selected pile of clothing and donned a wrinkled flannel shirt with a Salsa Grenade tie, an over-large Harris tweed jacket, shapeless lilac cords and steel-toed boots. Heavy framed spectacles with milk-bottle lenses completed the ensemble. He stood before a mirror and combed his hair from back to front. Satisfied, he moved over to the bed and assembled his handwritten papers. He patted the pockets of his jacket, producing a rattle that sounded as if he might be carrying lots of little bottles. He took a deep breath and read the words in the manner of an opera singer at rehearsal. 'Zsa, zsa-zsa, zsa,

zsa-zsa, zsa-zsa . . . A MUZZLE ON THEE . . . zsa-zsa . . . MY SANITY . . .'

Murdo strutted and shook his head and hands at length, occasionally taking the box out, slowly raising it to eye level and gazing at it adoringly. Eventually he slumped on the bed and read his script in silence.

Rachel, dressed in the scarlet cheongsam, split from knee to waist, glided in on stiletto heels. Raising her arms to pat her dark hair which was done up in a chignon, she vamped it up as she approached Murdo. He gazed at her, open-mouthed.

'Hello, sailor,' Rachel said.

'It's me, Rachel!'

'I know it's you, fool. What's with the get-up? Go over to the mirror there and take a swatch at how awful you look.'

'I've done that already. It's okay. It's all part of the plan.'

'What plan?'

'I'm resorting to deceit and cunning,' Murdo said, 'to get the dough.'

'Haven't you sold the van yet? What have you been doing all morning?'

'I'm not selling the van.'

Rachel dug the fingers of both hands under her hair at the scalp line, threw her head back and looked Murdo straight in the eye. 'Oh, aren't you?'

'No, I'm going to sell something else. Look, I've worked everything out in fine detail.'

Murdo handed her the script. Rachel glanced at the first page only. 'What's this supposed to be?'

'Read it.'

'Well, well, well. What a busy little pumpkin you've been!'

'Busy enough,' Murdo said. 'This'll work. I've pulled strokes like this before. Did I tell you about the time I sold my mother's cow to Duncan Macdonald? I asked him for the head and I stuck it in the peat bog?'

'And when the poor old soul realised the cow was missing,' Rachel said in tired tones, 'you showed her the head and told her the beast must have drowned.'

'I'm telling you, if we follow this script all our problems will be solved.'

Rachel put both palms down flat on the bottom of the bed, stiffened her arms, leaned forward and said, 'But where's the cow going to come from this time?'

'What are you talking about? What cow?'

'Whose head are you going to chop off this time?' Morag asked.

'I know I've written a cracking script. And I know what's going to happen when we act on it.'

'You've been so busy scribbling, you don't even think about anyone else in your life.'

'Such as you, I suppose.'

'Such as me. Where do you think I got this gear I'm wearing? Why do you think I've made the effort to look glamorous? You leave me up here with seventeen pounds to my name? You promise to get three hundred and fifty pounds? I go downstairs to speak to Suki, eh?'

'Suki?'

'The owner's wife. She gives me a break on the room and lets me stay another night for nothing.' She spoke softly. 'I'm looking forward to being with you.'

'What do you think of the script?'

'Have you memorised this?'

'Yes.'

'Okay. Go ahead. A. B. C.'

'What?'

'Anger . . . Blethers . . . and Catching.'

'Yeah.'

'Yeah, get on with it. Anger first.'

Murdo threw his head back, mouth agape, and jerkily rotated his head. With clenched fists crossed, he beat his ribs in the manner of someone trying to restore circulation to frozen hands. Rachel, looking off to the side and apparently indifferent to his convulsions, smothered a yawn and nodded once briskly. 'Next: Blethers.'

Murdo looked down, remained with his head bowed for a beat or two, then slowly raised his gaze. He was weeping and shouting. '. . . THOU BLACK-MOUTHED MAID, THE ONLY TREE IN THE GARDEN OF EYES . . . A MUZZLE ON THEE.' Murdo paused theatrically. 'WITH BOLD ASSUR-ANCE YOU BENT ME TO YOUR WILL AND GNAWING DOUBT YOU BANISHED FROM MY HEART, AND SO ON THE SMOOTH PRE-DESTINED PATH OF MY YOUTH I MOVED THROUGH EACH DAY AND MY SENSE IM-BIBED THEIR SAP.' He sobbed uncontrollably and laid his head on folded arms.

After a long pause Rachel murmured, without looking at him, 'Try and get a little more volume, Murdo.'

'Huh?'

'A bit more like Pavarotti.'

'Pavarotti?'

'I'm only winding you up. Now, C for Catching.'

Murdo reached into his pocket and pulled out the jewellery box. He slowly raised it to eye level, opened the lid and gazed at the contents. His arms began to quiver with tension. With a strangled animal-like cry he lost his grip of the box and it flew six feet or so in the air to be caught one-handed by Rachel.

'Ugh . . . Oh!'

Rachel tossed the box back to him and he stuffed it in his pocket.

'Have you got the pills?'

Murdo slapped his jacket pocket. 'Yes.'

'Well, do you want the truth?'

'Yes.'

'The script's not bad.' She handed it back to him.

'The script's not bad? It's outstandingly good.'

'You make a pretty good fool.' She embraced him.

'If you deliver the lines I've written for you, Rachel, there's no way in the world we can fail to con anybody.'

'That'll depend on the guy you pick.'

'I've already picked him.'

'Who?'

There was a brief pause. Both spoke simultaneously: 'Sam the Scam!'

'Okay. Enough's enough.' Murdo abruptly disengaged himself from her embrace and marched purposefully to the doorway. 'I'm leaving you now and I may be gone for some time.'

11

Stalking

Murdo stood beside the notice board at the entrance to the pier. His whole body stiffened. Rachel was running at full pelt towards him. She wore a nurse's uniform with a little white cap on her head. 'Murdo, Murdo,' she shouted almost out of breath.

'What's up?'

'Murdo, you're behaving like a madman.'

'It's got to be done.'

'You're not going to go through with this nonsense, are you?'

'You bet . . . What are you doing here anyway?'

'I don't . . . I want to . . . You need help. You can't do this on your own.'

'Oh, yes I can. But you're welcome to tag along, if you want to see me taking the piss out of the man from Etive Television.'

'I can't let you do this on your own. I'm here to help.'

'Do you think I can't beat him?'

'Well . . .'

Murdo slashed the air with the script. 'Because,' he said, 'he's going to get whipped, kicked, trampled and thrashed.'

74

'Stop that kind of talk. It *is* terrific being with you. You're a very attractive man, you know?'

'I know, I know.'

'Let me know honestly how you feel.'

'I'm feeling powerful.'

Rachel moved swiftly behind him, slipping her arms through Murdo's armpits. 'Why did you pick Sam?' she said.

'Why? Because he's the guy who made *Our Land* and he's a big player.'

'Never mind that bloody programme. I don't want to talk about that just now. And neither do you.' After a brief pause, she placed her hands on his chest. 'Why did you pick Sam?'

'He has no respect for anyone but himself. As far as he's concerned, there are only two types of people in the world: those who are used by others and those who are able to use people. He thinks that I can be used, but he's got another think coming.'

'I'll help you.'

'Please yourself. I'll play him like a salmon on the hook.'

'Did you hear what I said? I'm going to help you.'

'Did *you* hear what *I* said? I'm going to pull this off on my own.'

Rachel let her hands run down his chest and leaned over him until her chin was resting on the top of his head. 'Murdo?'

'Mmmm.'

'What would you say if I told you I don't really care about the money?'

Murdo was preoccupied scanning the script. 'Do you think it would be over the top if I started spitting?'

'I'm spending the night . . . here.' Rachel settled herself against him even more cosily, until her bosom was up against the back of his head. 'How do you fancy a soft, warm bed yourself?'

'That would be very . . .' He paused. 'Listen, Rachel, I've got work to do. I'm not thinking about beds but of the glorious day that has dawned – the day that has always been my *destiny*.'

Murdo slumped down still further.

'Why don't we take a chance?' Rachel said. There was a slight pause. 'I'm willing.'

'But why did you suddenly lose interest in the money?

'Ohhh – two reasons. One, Suki has given us this room for nothing tonight. And two, I want you to be with me, Murdo.'

Suddenly somebody emerged from the Tartan Pagoda. He made for the door of a Range Rover and took out a brown leather briefcase.

'Look, Murdo, that's the guy we've been looking for.'

'Where? Who is it?'

'That half-wit in the baseball cap who's probably from Corstorphine but imagines he's in Hollywood – that's him on the other side of the Range Rover.'

They looked at Sam as he gave some instructions involving exaggerated hand gestures to the driver of the Range Rover. He turned away and moved briskly down the line of vehicles in the direction of the Bar Restaurant beyond. As he approached Rachel and Murdo, the couple turned their backs and pretended to read the ferry timetable.

'I recognise him,' Murdo said. A new thought occurred to him. 'Maybe he'll recognise me. I've been on television, you know?'

'Murdo, you've been on *Gaelic* television. *Speaking Our Language*. At half past four in the morning. Those Etive TV guys didn't see you. Nobody saw you. The odd member of your fan club maybe saw you, but that folded last year when two of them died.'

Murdo's head went down, his face crumpled and tears were not far away. 'There's no need for that, Rachel . . .'

Rachel spoke in exasperation. 'Look, when anybody comes home at the weekend and hears Gaelic on the telly, it's high time to get into the jammies. That means that it's really, really late.'

'I'm a semi-famous actor.'

'Semi-famous? You're an unknown, darling. Actually, you're not even an unknown. You're a fucking missing person!'

'I think you might be right,' Murdo said plaintively.

'I'm sorry, Murdo. It *is* terrific being with you. It's my fault, Murdo. I shouldn't have mentioned *Speaking Our Language*. You were terrific in that programme. First time round, they got thousands of letters singing your praises.'

'Really?'

'Really. Now, are you up for socking it to Etive Television?'

As Sam passed them Rachel extended her forefinger towards him and curled it as though squeezing a trigger. With an almost imperceptible nod of her head towards the retreating Sam, they casually followed their prey. They walked very slowly – this caused by Murdo's suddenly acquired ataxic gait – towards the entrance of the Bar Restaurant.

12

Showtime

24 August 2010, 1 p.m.

With Rachel in the lead, the pair made their way to the table occupied by Sam. He was busy with a bottle of Tippex, meticulously altering receipts with the small brush. When he saw how fetching Rachel looked in her nurse's uniform, his eyes almost popped out of his head. He hastily put down his tools and openly ogled her.

'May we join you?' Rachel said.

'Uh-huh,' Sam grunted.

A young Thai girl carrying a tray of dirty dishes passed them. She executed a formal bow and said, 'Kam sah ham ni da.'

'What's she saying?' Sam said.

'I suppose she's asking how the pig is,' Murdo said.

Sam looked at Murdo blankly, and then continued falsifying his receipts.

The Thai girl, carrying a notebook and pen, came up to the table. 'What you have?' she asked.

'A bottle of water and two glasses, please,' Rachel replied. She unbuttoned Murdo's jacket. 'Medication time, Angus.'

At the sound of her voice Sam looked up from his receipts.

Murdo was fiddling with an array of medicine bottles on the table.

Rachel acknowledged Sam's interest with a tight smile of apology. She half rose to accept the mineral water and glasses which the girl laid on the table. Placing her palms together and bringing the tips of her fingers up to her chin the waitress bowed. 'Welcome,' she said.

'Thank you,' Rachel said. 'God, I hope these new pills work. I'm just hoping that he doesn't have another one of his . . . *attacks*.'

When he heard this, Sam looked down at his papers. He glanced over at Murdo who was nervously tossing his head from side to side and snapping his teeth together, as though trying to bite his left ear. Suddenly, he emitted a high-pitched scream, shuffled his feet on the floor and, with clenched fists crossed, beat his ribs in the manner of someone trying to restore circulation to frozen hands.

Rachel was calmly opening the medicine bottles and measuring out an assortment of brightly coloured pills onto the table. She filled the glasses and held hers up. 'Good health,' she said.

Murdo chinked her glass with his own, crammed a fistful of pills into his mouth and gulped a mouthful of water. 'Goo' healsh . . . ish lo' liff.'

Sam leaned forward and indicated Murdo with a tilt of his head. 'What's wrong with him?'

Rachel tapped her breast. 'Heart.'

'Oh, right,' Sam said.

'His heart's knackered and there's nothing they can do for him.'

'I'm sorry to hear that.'

During this exchange, Murdo pulled a sheaf of papers

from his pocket, threw his head back, mouth agape, and jerkily rotated his head.

'He's just been discharged from hospital in Inverness this morning,' Rachel said.

'Was it Raigmore he was in?'

'No. He was in the asylum. He went bonkers when this girlfriend he had jilted him. Broke his heart.'

'. . . THOU BLACK-MOUTHED MAID, THE ONLY TREE IN THE GARDEN OF EYES . . . A MUZZLE ON THEE,' Murdo declaimed. He paused theatrically. 'WITH BOLD ASSURANCE YOU BENT ME TO YOUR WILL AND GNAWING DOUBT YOU BANISHED FROM MY HEART, AND SO ON THE SMOOTH PREDESTINED PATH OF MY YOUTH I MOVED THROUGH EACH DAY AND MY SENSE IMBIBED THEIR SAP.'

'I'm sorry, sir,' Rachel said, 'he's on about that damned woman again.'

Murdo got angrily to his feet. 'I'm getting rid of it! This damned thing is only a cancer to my soul!' Murdo yanked the ring-box out of his pocket and with both hands he held the box above his head. His arms were trembling with suppressed anger. 'Two thousand quid's worth . . . and it wasn't good enough for the bitch! Well, she wasn't good enough for me. I'm slinging it into the loch!'

'Put that ring away, Angus,' Rachel said.

With a strangled animal-like cry Murdo lost his grip of the box and it flew in the air to be caught clumsily by Sam. 'Ugh . . . Oh!'

As Rachel comforted Murdo who was weeping un-restrainedly by now, Sam opened the box and a flashy engagement ring was revealed. He was about to remove the ring from the velvet pad into which it was slotted when the fist of Rachel enfolded it and slipped it out of his hand. 'You keep that ring, Angus,' she said. 'It's worth money.'

Sam was interested.

'I don't care,' Murdo said. 'Let me throw it in the loch.'

'Look,' Rachel said, 'take it back to the shop you bought it in next time you're down in Glasgow. They'll give you half of what it's worth. You'll get a thousand back easy.'

Sam was even more interested. 'Can I see it, please?' he said.

'No!' Rachel said.

'What would he take for it?' Sam said. 'Three hundred?'

'No way!' Rachel said.

'Let him speak,' Murdo said.

Rachel stood up and grabbed her bag. 'Angus, listen to me,' she said. 'Your porch-light's gone out just now . . .'

Murdo had his forefingers stuck in his ears and his entire upper body was swaying violently from side to side.

'He looks perfectly sane to me,' Sam said.

'Aw, to hell with the pair of you!' Rachel said.

'I don't care . . . I'm going to sling it,' Murdo said. He stretched his hand out as though to retrieve the ring.

Sam pleaded. 'No, don't do that, Angus. I'll do you a favour. I'll give you . . . Uh, what will you take for it?'

'I don't care . . . make me an offer.'

'Well . . .' Sam said, lifting his case into full view,

opening it and taking out three bundles of money. 'What if I give you . . . Let's see . . .' He made a fan out of the notes and waved them in their faces.

'I don't care . . . I'll take anything. Five, twenty, fifty . . . whatever . . .'

Rachel placed her hand on top of Murdo's and addressed Sam. 'What the hell's going on? Is this you taking advantage of a poor soul who's had his heart broken?'

Murdo plucked the money from Sam's hands. In a lightning move, he thrust his hand into the briefcase and got another fistful of notes. He tossed all the money carelessly into Rachel's lap. 'You take the money, Rachel,' he said. 'I don't care.' Murdo seized the ring from Rachel and stuffed it into the breast pocket of Sam's jacket. 'You've got the ring now,' he said. 'And I've got the money.'

Sam tried to make a grab for the notes, but Rachel hid them behind her back.

'GIVE ME BACK THAT MONEY! IT'S MINE!'

'Wrong,' Murdo said. 'I understand how you feel, but you made a mistake. You thought I was just another loser to be used, and I'm not. I know the difference between right and wrong. You did wrong, darling. And I'm going to broadcast far and wide that I got the better of the man who made *Our Land*.'

Sam turned to Rachel. 'What do you have to say to the hero?'

'I'm just speechless,' Rachel said. She looked admiringly at Murdo. 'I'd say that's exactly what he is – a hero.'

'Okay. Okay. That's . . . So I'll, uh, say . . . that's it, then.'

'Beat it, you horrible creep,' Murdo said. 'You're only getting what's due you, and don't you be slagging off our folk. That programme was full of lies about us . . . Here's a health to the noble Gael . . . bullshit! We're just like everybody else – good and bad mixed. We've a saying in Uist: "When the lid of the pipe-box drops, the bullshit stops." We've just dropped the lid here. Play or walk.'

Rachel and Murdo watched him go out the door. Their faces broke into huge grins. They raised one fist triumphantly over their heads, punching the air like winning prize fighters.

13

Rachel's revenge

24 August 2010, 2 p.m.

Rachel and Murdo were giggling and laughing in turns as they drove out of Uig, Rachel at the wheel of the van.

'What do you think will happen,' Murdo said, 'when he finds out the ring's from Woolies?'

'You're terrific at recognising them, though.'

'Stick with me – you haven't seen anything yet,' Murdo chuckled.

When Rachel steered the van into a passing-place on the right-hand side of the road and came to a halt he raised his voice. 'Why did we stop here?'

'We want to send our last farewell to Sam the Scam.' She pointed to the ship gliding smoothly below them in the bay.

'That's him leaving the island nearly a thousand pounds lighter,' Murdo said.

'Congratulations on how well you did in the restaurant,' Rachel said. 'Do you know this? I can't get over how bold you've become.'

'What do you mean – "bold"?'

'Well, you were sitting there in the restaurant and you were about to launch an *attack* on Sam the Scam.'

'Yes.'

'You didn't feel the slightest bit afraid . . .'

'Why should I feel afraid?' Murdo said. 'Listen, I used to go to dances in Eochar, get into fights with the local boys and the Loch Carnan folk. Survive that and you'll survive anything.'

'Murdo, I was afraid he'd eat you alive. There'd be nothing left of you but bones . . . and a hank of hair.'

'Wheesht, girl,' Murdo said. 'Stop your idle talk. That's himself away now.'

'Good riddance,' Rachel said. In one swift movement she plucked the spectacles from Murdo's face, threw them casually out the window and gave him a great big kiss.

Murdo blushed. 'What are we doing now?'

'We'll go right now.'

'Are we heading straight for Glasgow?'

'Portree.'

'Why?'

'First thing, we're going to buy a new outfit for you. You're just an untidy old midden, Murdo. You look like a tsunami survivor.'

'Then we go to Glasgow?'

'No,' Rachel said, 'we're going back to the Tartan Pagoda. Surely you remember, Murdo, the night of a thousand kisses?'

Murdo did not say a word. Eventually he spoke. 'That's it, then?'

'No,' Rachel said, 'I've business to attend to in the town as well.'

'What kind of business?'

'I'm going to phone two or three people I know.'

'Male or female?' Murdo said, a note of jealousy in his voice.

'I suppose they'll be male,' Rachel said, smiling.

'Who are they?'

'Reporters.'

'What do you mean?' Murdo said. 'You say you're going to phone newspaper people you know. Yet you're not sure whether they're male or female. Who can make any sense out of that?'

'Can't fool you, Murdo, eh?' Rachel said. 'I should've said that I knew the *numbers* of some local newspapers. I'll give Oban, Stornoway and Portree a bell and I'll tell him – or her – about the scandal.'

'What good will that do?'

'Allow me to tell you something about news gatherers, in print, on radio or on television,' Rachel said. She drew a deep breath. 'News men – can't live with them, but also, unfortunately, can't live without them.

'If it's Lachie Macdonald who gets himself into bother because of his liking for booze, women, young boys or any other addiction, newspaper men don't give a fig. But if you have fame that'll make a difference. They'll go off in a frenzy. Imagine what it'd be like if you were George Michael or Wayne Rooney and you broke the law *and* a reporter found out about it . . . well, they'd be at you in a flash.

'And below these guys there's a veritable army of people who have to be careful. If you work in the media, for example, if you do the wrong thing, and if people find out about it, you'll be harassed.'

'Even a director in Gaelic television?' Murdo said.

'Oh, the people are going to find out about Sam,' Rachel said. 'Definitely.'

'No one ever said you didn't have a fast mouth on you, Rachel.'

86

'Thank you,' Rachel said. 'My father says it's part of my natural charm.'

'Well, you were misled by your father,' Murdo said, 'but never mind that, how is your tongue going to help you?'

'I'm going to tell the local papers first.'

'What are you going to tell them?'

'That I saw with my own two eyes almost four thousand pounds in his briefcase. I'll say it isn't proper for a director to be running around with that kind of cash. Something weird's going on. They ought to interview Sam, and also it'd be prudent to find out about the carry-on with Suki and Nigel.

'Most of the time it's from the little newspapers that the big boys get their stories anyway. The people who are most vulnerable to those vultures are the ones who've gained a degree of fame in their chosen professions – footballers, golfers, boxers, pop stars, writers, academics. Most nine-to-five folk think that these guys get too much money for what they do – even their fans, so when they read the stories in the papers or see them on telly or online, they shudder, but deep down they'll be happy.'

'And they'll need, these famous people, an able lawyer, won't they?' Murdo said. 'Somebody like you perhaps?'

'Perhaps,' Rachel said.

'So Sam'll get clobbered by the media.'

'That's not all. Our local hero won't have the red carpet rolled out for him when he heads home to Perth. Pity Etive Television where he's heading.'

'Why?' Murdo said.

'TV executives abhor financial malfeasance. The MD

will say, "Samuel, you're like a lump of burning white phosphorus. You've made yourself *radioactive*. If we retain you in the job, not a cheep will come out of the phones. If the advertisers find out that someone in our company has been skimming money, they'll stop giving us money. And we'll all be in the poor house."'

'What happens then?' Murdo said.

'The Board will release a press statement.'

'What will they say in it?'

'They'll lie. The MD will say, "It is with regret that Etive Television announces the departure of BAFTA-winning director, Sam Kerr. Mr Kerr is seeking fresh challenges in other fields. We are obliged to say that we wish him well as he moves on." And that's it.'

'What a box-up Sam made!' Murdo said. 'I mentioned the Eochar dances a while back. They were seriously brutal. All punches and cracking noises. The following day an old guy used to creep around the pathway to the hall collecting teeth and putting them in a jam-jar – I don't know what he needed them for – and I thought we had a pretty tough life. But when I hear about life in the media, Eochar was only a picnic.'

'Come on, Murdo,' Rachel said, 'you and I are going on a picnic. Portree first, then back to Uig where you'll get your heart's desire.'

14

Murdo has doubts

In Room 5 of the Tartan Pagoda Suki stood motionless by the bed. She was cradling a large cardboard box, wrapped in gaily coloured paper and bedecked in tartan ribbon in her arms. Gracefully she placed the box on the bed. She stood back to admire the effect and brought her hands together, once, in a girlish gesture of approval.

Rachel's voice was heard from outside. 'Stop it, Murdo.'

From outside the door Murdo said, 'I'm about done in, Rachel.'

Murdo staggered into the room carrying Rachel over his shoulder in a parody of a bridegroom on his honeymoon night. He was breathing heavily, faint in the body and weak in the legs. He addressed Suki breathlessly. 'Out of my way, lady . . . before I peg out.'

Suki stepped smartly to the side, and Murdo staggered past her and unceremoniously dumped a giggling Rachel onto the bed.

'Mind the present!' Suki said.

Rachel scrambled to her knees and placed a hand on the box. 'Oh, you've brought us a present, Suki? That's exceedingly kind of you. Isn't it, Murdo?'

'What is it?' Murdo said.

'Open it and see,' Suki said.

Rachel tore the wrapping paper from the box excitedly. 'I think I know what's inside this box.' To Murdo she said, 'Wait till you see this, Murdo.' She pulled out layers and layers of packing material and eventually took out a leather case. Puzzled, she slowly opened the case and a camera was revealed. She looked enquiringly at Suki.

'We call it a camera,' Suki said. She glared at Rachel and Murdo in mock exasperation. 'What a pair of mouth-breathers you two are! I'm not giving it to you. I'm going to take some pictures with it . . . tonight . . . of you pair in bed together! Aw, don't worry, I'll not get in your way. I'll just stand up on the dresser over there.'

Rachel and Murdo stared in horror at Suki, their mouths open. There was a long pause. Finally, all three burst out laughing.

'It's for you, Murdo,' Suki said. 'I was very proud of you down there. There's a young Thai girl working in the bar I'm pretty friendly with. I went over for a gab with her and I was there when you sorted Sam out.'

'Thanks very much indeed,' Murdo said. 'Now, Suki, will you excuse us? Rachel and I have to be alone for a while . . .'

'Tell me about it!' Suki said. 'I'm working downstairs in the bar, I see a young couple on one of the love-seats, she's sitting on his lap, and they're sooking the faces off one another . . . I feel like going up to them and saying "Hey, do you mind if I join you? It's been so long!"'

Rachel had a smile on her face. 'Goodbye, Suki . . . And I'm deeply obliged to you. I've learned a lot from you. We can close our eyes and dream of whatever'll make us feel better.' She gestured towards herself and Murdo. 'But this is the heart of the matter. This is what it all boils down to. Female and male together, and that's it.'

Suki bowed gracefully, her hands in the prayer position.

'Suki?' Murdo said.

'Yes?'

Murdo produced a full wallet and handed some banknotes over to her. 'Could you possibly bring us up a bottle of champagne?'

Suki ignored the money and exited smoothly.

Murdo shrugged and moved over to sit on the edge of the bed.

Rachel took hold of his hand. 'She's lonely, Murdo,' she said. 'I feel sorry for her.'

'She's not the only one.'

Rachel, excited, seized both Murdo's hands in her own. 'I'm going to show you something, Murdo.'

'You are?'

'Yes, I'm going to show you how you can have a conversation between yourself and the hidden Murdo deep inside you.'

'Okay, what do we do?'

'Close your eyes, love.'

'They're closed.'

'Allow your mind to drift with the wind . . . slowly, flowingly . . . just as morning dew departs from the greensward at sunrise . . .'

'Is that it?'

'Wheesht! Repeat after me: What would you have me do?'

'What would you have me do?'

'Again, Murdo, say after me: Where would you have me go?'

'Where would you have me go?'

A slight pause ensued.

'What would you have me say, and to whom?'

'What would you have me say, and to whom?' Murdo sighed.

There followed a longer pause.

Rachel released his hands. 'Are you okay?' she said.

Silence reigned.

Finally, Murdo spoke. 'Yes, I'm okay.'

'Are you sure you want to go ahead with this?' Rachel said.

'I'm not sure of anything.'

'I am,' Rachel said. 'I know exactly what I've got to do.'

'If you want to know what's troubling me the most about all this,' Murdo said, 'I'll tell you. You and I are going to make love presently. Then, in the morning, we'll go to Uist. I'll be running to Creagorry every day for a bottle of rum for the old man. You'll be in the bosom of your family for a few days, then you'll go back to university in Glasgow and I'll be left – a man almost forty years of age – a laughing-stock, an object of mockery, an object of pity . . . to you, Rachel, and to your pals.'

'Listen . . .'

'This is not the way I want things to be,' Murdo said. 'Oh, sure, I want to go to bed with you. But it's what's going to happen afterwards, that's what's worrying me.'

'I don't . . . I don't know what to say to you,' Rachel said.

'Rachel, why are you doing this?'

'Doing what?'

'I'm only a pleasant diversion to you, Rachel, right? Your future is all mapped out. And there's no place for someone like me in it.'

'I've gone over this a hundred times,' Rachel said. 'What my parents want to do is control my life. The Rachel inside me wants her freedom. They're expecting me home tomorrow. I don't have the heart to face that.'

'Christ, your home's only two hours away.'

'I'm not going to Uist. I'm going straight down to Glasgow.'

'But you'll lose if you do that . . . your father and mother . . . me.'

'Maybe I'll lose something . . . but I'll gain something far more valuable. I'll be free.'

'Free? Did you consider anyone else?'

'My own needs, whatever they are, must come first, Murdo. If I'm not happy – if I'm forced to do things against my will – then I can't make anyone else happy.'

Murdo stood up and walked on weak joints across to the dresser.

15

The Eriskay Giant

24 August 2010, 10.10 p.m.

'Seems to me I can hear a kind of selfish rap to that, Rachel,' Murdo said. 'Me, me, me, who's more important than me? I'd say you don't mind riding roughshod over the feelings of others.'

'Come here, Murdo. Please don't go away from me.'

'Is this the best you can do for your parents? Is this the best you can do for me? You'll give a night's relief to a guy who's old enough to be your father, and then you'll abandon all of us?'

'Wrong!' Rachel said. 'You've read it all wrong, Murdo.'

'At least tell me the truth. How do you really feel about me? Are you attracted to me only because I'm weak and you can control me easily?'

'No!'

'Because I've got news for you, girl,' Murdo said. 'I'm undergoing some kind of process of change. You know, I'm liberated, as well as being sober? And it's a good feeling.'

'Murdo,' Rachel said, 'do you think you'll be buried in Nunton cemetery?'

'What's that got to do with it?'

'Do you think you'll ever leave your old man, the Benefits office and the blow-outs at weddings and dances in Eochar Hall?'

Murdo sighed. 'I'll have to leave all of that stuff behind some time. I'd go tomorrow . . . if I had a choice.'

'You have a choice, Murdo,' Rachel said. 'Come with me to Glasgow. I'm not going back to university either. I'll get a job. I'll support you. You're the one who should be going to university, Murdo.'

They were quiet for a while.

Murdo broke away from the dresser and went back towards the bed. 'You have to do something first,' he said.

'I'm more than willing. Come on, Murdo, give me a hug.'

'That's only part of it. You have to do something else.'
'What?'

'You have to marry me,' Murdo said. He stopped talking. 'I don't have a ring . . . I had one but . . .'

This made Rachel laugh. 'If that's what you want . . . Okay.'

'Don't just say "okay" as though I've just offered you a cup of tea,' Murdo said. 'At times I don't understand you, Rachel. I don't know what's happening to us. I spoke to . . . er, to the Murdo deep inside me just as you asked me to – and the answer I got was that I shouldn't touch you without getting your commitment to marry me. Isn't there some little shred of hope for us?' Murdo sat down on the edge of the bed and placed his hands on her shoulders. 'Oh, my darling,' he said softly.

'I'll never hurt you, Murdo,' Rachel said. 'That's exactly how I'm feeling just now, and I don't know what else to tell you.' She stroked his cheek with the back of her hand.

Then, Murdo, in slow motion, drew the duvet back. He stood up straight and started to take off his clothes. 'Oh, Rachel . . .'

Someone knocked timidly on the door. Murdo and Rachel were oblivious. They looked at each other lovingly.

'We'll live together in Glasgow, eh?' Rachel whispered.

Murdo nodded in assent and removed his trousers. The knocking on the door resumed, louder this time.

'I love you, Murdo,' Morag said.

'I love *you*, Rachel.' Murdo said. He was about to leap into the bed with Rachel when Morag teetered into the room, carrying a bottle of champagne and flute glasses on a tray.

As soon as she opened her mouth it was clear that she been indulging in mood-altering substances. 'Oh, it's love . . . As Neruda once said . . .'

'The Nerudas have it easy,' Murdo said. 'They get all the building work in the islands.'

Morag carried on speaking. 'As Neruda once said . . .'

'Oh, champagne!' Rachel said. 'Isn't that wonderful, Murdo! I'd really adore a glass of it just now.'

'As Neruda once said . . .'

'You can drink the whole bottle,' Murdo said to Rachel. 'I'll stick to tap water.'

'As Alasdair MacAulay once said . . .'

'Alasdair MacAulay?' Rachel said. 'What happened to Neruda?'

'You're so ignorant,' Morag said, 'that neither of you wanted to hear what Neruda said.'

Murdo smiled indulgently at the women. 'Okay, what did Alasdair MacAulay say then?'

'He said that there were three things that we must take care of: a suckling babe, a poor widow and a barn door.'

Rachel spoke as though what she had heard was a source of wonder to her. 'Did he say that? That's pretty funny. I don't know what it has to do with anything, but I like it. I'm just going to say this in the passing – it's high time you took a holiday . . . for at least a month.'

'Oh,' Morag said, 'I'm going on one very soon . . . to Stornoway!'

Murdo was growing impatient. He held his trousers in the fig-leaf position. With difficulty he extracted a bundle of notes from a pocket and thrust it into her fist.

'Here, take this,' he said. 'I hope you enjoy Stornoway . . . A good thing is worth waiting for.'

'From your lips to God's ears!' Morag said.

Suddenly she fell silent. It was as though she had been struck by lightning. She examined Murdo carefully. It was obvious as she looked at him from top to toe, with her head bobbing up and down, that she was trying to gauge how tall he was.

'What did you say just then?' she said, almost chok-ing.

'When?' Murdo said.

'Murdo, hurry up,' Rachel said in a plaintive voice.

'A good thing is . . .'

'A good thing is worth waiting for?' Murdo said.

'A good thing is worth waiting for!' Morag said in a squeaky voice. She was almost delirious. 'Those are the blessed words! You've got it! The Lord Himself sent you my way!'

Rachel squeezed her head under the pillow and said in a muffled voice, 'Aw, no! Get rid of her, Murdo.'

Murdo propelled the old lady who was still babbling towards the door. 'We'll talk about all this in the morning . . . Have a nice mug of Horlicks . . . Come on, now . . . Good night, sleep tight . . . You'll feel a lot better after forty winks . . .' He closed the door and turned the key.

Morag railed excitedly at him from the corridor. 'I know who you are. You're the Eriskay Giant. Did you bring my money?'

Murdo was confused. He scratched his head and walked over to the bed.

'The Eriskay Giant?' Rachel said. 'Well, big boy, come on over here till we see if the poor soul's telling the truth.'

Murdo turned off the light and slipped smoothly into the bed. All that could be heard were soft murmurs and the rustling of bedclothes in the blackness.

Epilogue

Morag has gone to the demnition bow-wows since she
returned to Stornoway. She's drinking more and more.
She has a nice wee flat in The Cairns in which she drinks
a litre of vodka every single day. The taxi drivers who
run the cutter for her call her 'The Pension Plan'.

John, with his bullhorn in his hand, can still be seen
around Uig pier. Make sure, if you spit when he's
around, you don't lick your lips after it.

Nigel is still a man who spends his days not doing very
much. Last year he sold six of his Jesus or Frank Bruno
statuettes.

Suki is making a fortune in the Tartan Pagoda. She's
crammed a team of Thai girls into a caravan round the
back, and every night a couple of them, taking turns,
perform lap dancing in the Cocktail Bar.

Murdo is as happy as a sand boy. At university, he's
heavily involved in politics and President of the Debat-
ing Society, Student Senate. This doesn't leave much
time for study. However, he's doing his best. He almost
had a slip at Christmas time. He put a lot of work into a

paper for the Sociology lecturer. When he found out it was worth only a Beta Minus he was bitterly disappointed. He went on a drinking bout that night. The following day he realised that his life was slipping towards the toilet again, and he did the right thing. He sobered up. He went to the lecturer and asked him where he was going wrong. The guy gave him some tips to improve his writing skills. Since then, he has been on the wagon and his grades have improved significantly.

Rachel is having a rather bumpy ride just now. Recently she's been phoning and writing to her parents. When they ask her what she meant when she told them there was to be an addition to the family, she tells them she's *not* pregnant and that she hopes to bring a boyfriend home with her at the end of term. What she doesn't tell them is that it's not Murdo who'll be along with her but a tall, dark and handsome young man whom she met at the university. His name is Said Khan.

Dolina, the loopy old woman Sam was courting, is now back at home. She's kept awfully busy writing letters to a young guy who's in Barlinnie just now doing an eight-year stretch for culpable homicide. They expect to get married in 2015 when he'll be released and she'll be seventy years of age.

Sam dropped out of sight after his summons to a board meeting of Etive Television directors. Rumours persisted, however, that he was on the streets selling *The Big Issue* and that he was detoxing in some kind of hostel. No reliable information could be found about him until it was reported that he had been seen in the Caberfeidh

Hotel in Stornoway at the time of the National Mod. It seems that he, Murdo Morrison of MGAlba and Margaret Mary Murray of BBCAlba – both members of the Committee for the Support of Gaelic Media – were whispering in a corner until the wee small hours. He has a new nickname: Lazarus.